Alexander blew out the last candle.

We were in total darkness. I couldn't see Alexander, the mouth of the cave, or even my own fingers.

Alexander kissed the back of my hand, slowly pecking his way up my arm until he reached my neck.

I paused. "What is the surprise?" I asked. "Are we on sacred ground?"

"Want to find out?" he asked. "Wait one minute."

A surprise, I thought. *What could it be?*

I felt a warm grasp on my neck.

It was then that I knew. My fantasy was finally coming true. Alexander was going to bite me.

My heart began to pulse against the flesh of his palm. I started to visualize my new life as his hand lay on my most vital of veins.

My dream was to become a vampire, for Alexander to be the one who turned me and be the one to whom I'd be bonded for eternity. But as he held my neck, I suddenly wasn't sure if I was ready to plunge myself into the darkness forever.

ALSO BY ELLEN SCHREIBER

Ellen Schreiber

Vampire Kisses 4

Dance with a Vampire

KATHERINE TEGEN BOOKS
An Imprint of HarperCollins Publishers

Katherine Tegen Books is an imprint of HarperCollins Publishers.

Vampire Kisses 4: Dance with a Vampire
Copyright © 2007 by Ellen Schreiber

www.harperteen.com

Library of Congress Cataloging-in-Publication Data
Schreiber, Ellen.
    Vampire kisses 4 : dance with a vampire / Ellen Schreiber.—1st. ed.
        p.   cm.
    Summary: When a preteen vampire appears in Dullsville, Goth-girl Raven must
protect her younger brother and her own relationship with her vampire boyfriend,
Alexander.
    ISBN 978-0-06-177898-8
    [1. Vampires—Fiction. 2. Brothers and sisters—Fiction.] I. Title: Vampire kisses
four. II. Title: dance with a vampire. III. Title.
PZ7.S3787 Vamd 2007   2006028532
[Fic]—dc22   CIP
                                                                                 AC

Typography by Sasha Illingworth
09 10 11 12 13 LP/RRDH   10 9 8 7 6 5 4 3
❖
Revised paperback edition, 2009

Many fangs
to my brother Mark
for your invaluable help, guidance, and generosity

CONTENTS

"I know what you're thinking . . ."
—Valentine Maxwell

I awoke from a deadly slumber entombed in Alexander's coffin.

Since arriving at the Mansion shortly before Sunday morning's sunrise, I'd been lying next to my vampire boyfriend, Alexander Sterling, as he slept the weekend sunlit hours away, hidden in the closet of his attic room.

This was a dream come true. My first real taste—or in this case, bite—of the vampire lifestyle.

We nestled in my true love's bed—a claustrophobic black wooden casket. I was as blind as any bat; we could have been buried in the deepest recesses of a long-forgotten cemetery. Encased in our compacted quarters, I could easily touch the closed lid above me and brush my elbow against the side wall. The sweet scents of pine and cedar floated around me like incense. I couldn't see anything, not even my own black-fingernailed hand. No sounds were audible from outside the coffin. Not a siren, a bird, or the howling wind. I even lost track of time. I felt like we were the only two people in the world—that nothing existed outside these confining coffin walls.

Blanketed by darkness and a soft-as-a-spider's-web goose-feathered duvet, I was enveloped in Alexander's arctic white arms, my head gently resting against his chest. I felt his warm breath against my cheek. I imagined his deadly pale lids covering his chocolate brown eyes. I playfully fingered his velvet lips and brushed my fingertips over his perfect teeth until I felt one as sharp as a knife.

I tasted my finger for blood. Unfortunately, there was none.

I was so close to being part of Alexander's world—forever.

Or was I?

Though it was Sunday and I was exhausted from having spent the past few weeks protecting my nemesis, Trevor Mitchell, from the fangs of twin vampires, Jagger and Luna Maxwell, I was restless. I couldn't change my sleeping pattern from night to day.

Cuddling close to Alexander and sharing his world, I wanted nothing more than to spend our time kissing, playing, and talking.

But as he slept tranquilly, I could only think of one thing: A preteen vampire had descended upon Dullsville. And his name was Valentine.

The younger brother of the nefarious Nosferatu twins had arisen from his own petite coffin a few days before from somewhere in the vampire world and had been spotted in Dullsville by my brother and his nerd-mate, Henry.

I could only presume what Valentine looked like based on my brother's description: pale skin, pierced ears, black fingernails. I imagined a smaller version of Jagger—cryptic, gaunt, ghastly. How cruel it was that Jagger's sibling was just like him, and mine the polar opposite of me. If only I had been blessed with a ghoulish little brother. We'd have spent our childhood chasing ghosts in Dullsville's cemetery, searching Oakley Woods for creepy spiders, and playing hide-and-shriek in our basement. Instead, I grew up with a brother who'd prefer to dissect square roots alone rather than dissect gummi worms together.

I wondered why Valentine suddenly showed up in the conservative town of Dullsville, far away from his Romanian homeland. Now that Alexander and I were free from the older Maxwell siblings, I'd set forth on a new mission—finding out the eleven-year-old Valentine's whereabouts and motives and keeping him from Billy Boy before it was too late. But during the sunlight hours, my brother and Dullsville were in no danger, so my mind strayed back to the only vampire I felt secure with.

As Alexander and I lay in the dark, entombed and entwined, I stroked his silky black hair.

There was no place for me in the daylight without him. I had accepted the dangers Alexander had so warned me about, but I couldn't spend an eternity in the scorching sun minus my true love. Didn't Alexander know how easily I could adapt to his world, sleeping together in our cozy casket, flying together in the night sky, living in the dusty old Mansion? I wondered what type of vampire I'd be: A gentle dreamer like Alexander or a bloodthirsty menace like Jagger? Either way, since Jagger and Luna had departed from Dullsville, Alexander and I finally had a chance to share our mortal and immortal worlds. However, there could be an obstacle in my way, now that Valentine was in town.

Alexander stirred. He, too, couldn't sleep.

"You're awake," he whispered sweetly. "I'm sure it must be hard for you to adjust your sleep schedule."

I didn't want to admit that I couldn't be the perfect vampiress.

"I can't rest with you so close to me. I feel more alive than ever," I said.

My fingers felt around his smooth face and found his soft lips. I leaned in to kiss him, but my nose accidentally bumped into his.

"I'm sorry," I said with a giggle.

"One of the drawbacks of dating a mortal," he teased, a smile in his voice. "But it's worth it."

"What do you mean?"

Instead of answering, he lightly touched my cheek, sending tingles through my body.

Then he pressed his lips to mine and raced his fingers down my spine. I thought I was going to die. My hair flopped in my face, and he did something I couldn't fathom doing in the dark.

He gently brushed it away.

I gasped.

"How did you know my hair was hanging in my eyes?"

Alexander didn't answer.

"You can see!" I said blindly. "You can see me."

"I'm very lucky," he finally admitted. "You happen to be quite beautiful."

There were so many mysteries to Alexander, I wondered how many more would be revealed to me—and how I could unlock them.

I buried my head in his chest as he gently caressed my back.

"The sun has set," he said matter-of-factly.

"Already? How can you tell?" I asked. "You can see that, too?"

But he didn't answer.

I could hear Alexander lift the coffin lid. He grabbed my hand and I reluctantly rose, standing in total darkness.

Alexander scooped me up in his arms and carried me out of the casket like Dracula holding his mortal bride. He gently lowered me and I hung close to him, unaware of our exact location. The doorknob squeaked and the closet door creaked open. I squinted as my eyes tried to adjust to the beam of moonlight that pierced the room.

We pulled on our combat boots as I sat on his beat-up comfy chair and Alexander knelt on the uneven hardwood floor.

"So, will you teach me to fly?" I asked, half teasing.

"Valentine is not the kind of boy Billy should be hanging out with. We must get to your brother before Valentine does."

With that, Alexander locked the closet door, grabbed my hand, and, for now, closed the portal to the Underworld.

* * *

Now that darkness had fallen over Dullsville, it was imperative that Alexander and I find Billy Boy; but I was torn. Today had been my first time really experiencing life as a vampiress. I never actually thought I'd get to spend the daylight hours in a coffin with a vampire. I didn't want it to end. As we reached Alexander's attic-room door, I paused.

"We need to leave," he said.

"I know."

I imagined my life with Alexander, his easel in one corner, my dresser adorned with Hello Batty figures in another. At night we'd wander the cemetery, hand in hand. We'd watch *Halloween* on his big-screen TV and follow specters in the hallways of his horribly desolate creaky Mansion.

Alexander extended his hand. I reluctantly let him lead me away from my dream world. We walked through the candlelit Mansion, past the huge rooms with sky-high ceilings, the wind whispering through the corridor.

At the foot of the red-carpeted grand staircase we greeted Alexander's butler, Jameson, who looked especially creepy today in his vintage black suit. He must have been staying out with his new girlfriend, my former boss Ruby White. His eyes were extra buggy, but his ghost white face blushed red when he spoke.

"Good evening, Miss Raven," he said softly in his Romanian accent.

"Hello, Jameson."

"I'll have dinner for you in a few moments," the creepy man said.

"I appreciate it, Jameson, but we don't have time for

that now," Alexander commented, like Batman to his butler, Alfred.

I felt a pang of loneliness for Jameson—he would have to eat alone in the Mansion.

Jameson looked relieved, though, and as we gathered our jackets, I could hear him on the telephone. "Miss Ruby? I'm available for dinner earlier than I thought . . . Wonderful. Yes, I would be grateful if you could pick me up here. I love a woman in charge," he teased.

I felt like we were traveling cross-country as Alexander drove us in Jameson's Mercedes down the twisty, winding, desolate roads away from Benson Hill to the immaculately manicured streets of my suburban neighborhood.

Anxious to find Billy Boy, I raced up the front steps and fumbled with my collection of keys—a house key, one front and one back door, a file drawer key, a diary key, and a few that I couldn't recall what they unlocked. All were attached to several key chains—an Olivia Outcast figure, a Hello Batty stuffie, and a plastic *Donnie Darko* picture.

My hands shook as I tried to find the right one.

Alexander calmly placed his hand on mine, his black plastic spider ring catching the moonlight, and took the faux barbed-wire key ring from me.

He quickly picked out my house key and put it in the lock.

Within a moment, we were inside.

"Billy Boy?" I called from the bottom of the stairs.

There was no answer. Not even a "Go away."

I turned to Alexander. He looked worried.

I flew up the beige-carpeted stairs and headed toward Billy Boy's room. A haphazardly painted sign with red-and-black letters hung on his closed door. "NO GHOULS ALLOWED. THAT MEANS YOU, RAVEN!"

I snarled and threw open the door.

"We need to talk," I warned.

Everything—desk, computer, computer games, sports posters, unmade bed—was in place in my brother's bedroom. Except him.

I searched the bathroom and the neatly kept guest room, but no pesky sibling.

I bounced down the stairs to find the front door opening.

"Billy Boy?" I asked.

Instead, it was my mother, wearing a mauve Ralph Lauren sweater and gray pants, coming into the hallway.

"Well, hello, Alexander," she said, her eyes twinkling. "It's great to see you."

Alexander was always shy around my parents. "Hello, Mrs. Madison," Alexander replied, flipping his hair back nervously.

"I've told you, you can call me Sarah," she said with an almost schoolgirl giggle.

I rolled my black-eye-shadowed eyes. I wasn't sure if my mother was happy that someone in Dullsville, much less the world, would accept me or if it was Alexander's mesmerizing chocolate eyes that were making her giddy. Or maybe she was having vivid flashbacks from her hippie days.

There wasn't enough time or therapy to figure it out.

"I'm so glad you both are here," she said sweetly. "I

just called you at Alexander's—"

"Is Billy coming home soon?" I interrupted.

"No, that's why I thought it would be a great opportunity for us to have dinner together. Just the four of us."

I sighed. Finally, after all these years of nagging me about the way I dressed, my mother was treating me like a young adult. Unfortunately for me, I couldn't revel in my chance to be indoctrinated into the circle of parental acceptance. I had other things on my mind.

"I have to talk to Billy Boy."

"He's at Math Club," she said, grabbing a gray vest from the hall closet. "They rented out the library for the year-end party."

"I have to tell him something," I said.

"We have reservations at Francois' Bistro. Your father had to stop by the office and is meeting us there."

"Francois'?" Even though conservative Dullsville was as small as a golf hole, Francois' was on the opposite side of town, miles away from the library.

"How about the Cricket Club?" I recommended, suggesting a restaurant closer to Billy's location.

"You want to go to the Cricket Club?" she asked. "I didn't think you liked that restaurant."

"What's not to like? It's popular and fun," I said convincingly.

"That's exactly the reason I thought you detested it."

I bit my black lip.

"I'll call your father from the car. I think he has the restaurant on speed dial," she said as she grabbed her car keys and led us out the front door.

2

Vampire Feast

Like an uninspired artist's brushstroke across a landscape that screams of boredom and unoriginality, so is the typical American strip mall. Dullsville's was no exception, inhabited by an overpriced furniture showroom, a swank shoe outlet, a scrapbooking store, and the same women's clothing shops that populated every other strip mall. Scattered in the middle of the parking lot full of SUVs were several chain restaurants with insufferably long waiting lists, buzzing pagers, and portions the size of Montana.

The Cricket Club, an English pub on steroids, specialized in food and beverages from across the pond. On the dark, overly shellacked wooden walls hung framed pictures of vintage cricket matches and other memorabilia, including authentic jerseys, scorecards, and trophies.

Alexander and I entered the restaurant dressed as

usual—or, in our case, unusual—me in my combat boots, pleated rayon skirt, and trilayered Morbid Monkey tank tops, and Alexander in studded black cargo pants and a Mindfreak T-shirt. Naturally, we got stares from the preppy patrons, as if we had arrived at a cocktail party without an invitation.

My dad was standing at the bar in a white oxford shirt and khakis, his tie loosened, with a soda in one hand. He closed out his tab and came over to us.

"Hello, Alexander," he said, shaking my boyfriend's hand as if they were football players at a coin toss.

"Hi, Mr. Madison," Alexander managed to say.

"Call me Paul," my dad said, patting him on the shoulder.

"Okay . . . Paul," Alexander mumbled awkwardly.

"Hi, sweetheart," my dad said, hugging me, then greeted my mom with a kiss on the cheek.

"Your table is ready, Mr. Madison," an über-tan college-aged hostess said, holding menus in the shape of cricket bats.

For a moment, I paused. I was proud to have my hippie-turned-conservative parents embrace Alexander's and my unconventional ways. Maybe this meant my mom was finally ready to buy me black fishnet stockings and torn mesh tops instead of J.Crew sweaters. My dad might invite Alexander and me to a Nightshade concert instead of a game of tennis. But they were a long way off from really accepting the situation. I was dying to tell them our secret—that they were about to have dinner with a vampire!

The conservative patrons with their perfect haircuts and impeccably groomed children gazed at us as if Alexander and I were Swamp Thing 1 and Swamp Thing 2. I could see the horror in their crystal blue eyes as they prayed that their coiffed kids wouldn't grow up and put purple streaks in their blond hair.

I was hoping for a quiet booth in the corner, away from gossipmongers and gawkers—a place from which I could easily sneak out of the Cricket Club.

Instead, the hostess showed us to a table in the center of the restaurant.

We started to sit down, and my ultrapale boyfriend politely held out my chair for me. My dad quickly rose and followed Alexander's gentlemanly example for my surprised mother.

"The four of us should eat out more often," my mom said as we settled in. "Alexander brings out the best in your father."

Alexander and I were on display, as if we were in the spotlight on a Broadway stage. The soft candlelight couldn't mask the occasional lingering gaze or whispers from the other pubsters.

However, I had other things on my mind. Aside from worrying about being an outcast, I had to figure out how Alexander and I were going to get to the library before Valentine did.

Or maybe we were already too late. I imagined that, between the stacks of physics and calculus books, Valentine could be gnashing his fangs into my brother's neck. But I had to remain positive. It wasn't likely Valentine would risk being easily spotted. Or would he?

"This is quite a pleasure," my father said genuinely. "Order anything you like. Your mother's paying," he teased.

Just then a slight woman in a black DKNY pantsuit came over and stood beside our table. She had Trevor Mitchell's face. It was his mother.

"Hi, Sarah. Hi, Paul," Mrs. Mitchell said. Her smile stretched so wide that her pink lipstick started to crack.

Mrs. Mitchell studied Alexander, then me, mentally taking notes of anything she could report to her tennis friends.

"This is a coincidence seeing you here," my mother said.

"Or fate," Mrs. Mitchell corrected as she gazed at my boyfriend.

"Oh . . . you know Alexander Sterling," my mom began.

"No, I've seen him about town, but I haven't had the pleasure of meeting him face-to-face."

Mrs. Mitchell extended her thin, flawless hand, complete with a French manicure and flaunting more dazzling jewelry than a saleswoman on QVC.

Alexander quickly reached his own hand to hers. I felt like he was shaking the hand of the Wicked Witch of the West—without the green skin.

"I don't believe I've ever seen you out in daylight," she stated flatly.

When Alexander and his family moved to Dullsville, Trevor had begun the rumor that the Sterlings were vampires, fueled by Mrs. Mitchell's remarks. I didn't want to give my nemesis's mother any more ammunition for her gossipmongering. Apparently, neither did my mother.

"Alexander's homeschooled," my mother announced.

You go, Sarah Madison, I thought to myself.

"Trevor was seeing a girl from Romania," Mrs. Mitchell said, then turned to Alexander. "I believe she was a friend of yours."

Alexander shrugged his shoulders. "We lived in the same town as the Maxwells, but we didn't see one another much."

"Interesting," Mrs. Mitchell retorted. "Anyway, she seems to have suddenly disappeared."

Then Mrs. Mitchell glared at me and raised one brown-pencil-drawn eyebrow, as if I'd had something to do with Luna's departure—which I did.

"Well, it was great seeing you," my dad interjected, forcing an end to the horribly awkward conversation.

"Of course. Mr. Mitchell will be arriving soon and I must get back to my table before they take it away. It was a delight to see you all," she said, and headed back to her booth.

"Thank you," I mouthed to my father.

We all breathed a collective sigh of relief, for different reasons, as we placed our blue linen napkins on our laps.

As we perused the menus, I racked my brain for a plan.

Just then a bearded waiter came over, recited the specials with a fake English accent, and dashed off with our drink orders.

"Don't be shy, Alexander," my mother began. "Order whatever you like. They're known for their fish and chips and bangers and mash."

"Alexander loves steak," I suggested.

"Then order the steak. . . . This is great, isn't it? We really haven't had a chance to talk. Either you two are heading out for the night or we're surrounded by other parents at parties. It's great to have the chance for a private conversation."

"So what sports are you into?" my dad asked. "Football or basketball?"

I rolled my eyes. "Alexander's an artist, Dad. He's not into sports."

"Oh . . . ," my dad said, fidgeting in his seat, dumbfounded as to how he would communicate with another male now that the subject of athletics was off the table. "Uh . . . that's okay," he stammered. "Raven's mother used to draw sketches when we first dated."

"I didn't know that," I said.

"What do you draw?" Alexander asked eagerly.

"Oh, that was ages ago. I haven't touched a sketchbook in years. What is your medium?" she asked.

"Oil paint."

"What is your specialty?" my mom inquired.

"Portraits. Family. Memories," Alexander responded mysteriously.

"Vampires," I said proudly.

My parents paused. "I see you have a lot in common," my dad commented.

"Raven's exams are coming up," my mom began, fiddling with her silver bracelet. "She said you were already taking your homeschool exams?"

"Yes. I've completed them."

"That's very impressive. Maybe some of your study habits will rub off on Raven," my dad added.

"Dad!" I whined, sinking in my chair. "Maybe we could finish with the interrogation after we order."

"You're right," my father agreed. "I'm hungry."

The waiter returned with our drinks. "Ladies," the waiter said, holding his paper and pen.

"I'll take the Cricket burger, well done," I said.

"I'll have the fish and chips," my mother said with a smile.

"For the young gentleman?"

Alexander cleared his throat. "I'll have the rib-eye steak."

"How would you like that prepared?"

"Raw," Alexander said matter-of-factly.

My parents and the waiter looked at my boyfriend oddly.

"He means rare," I corrected. "Medium rare."

I could see Mrs. Mitchell's head lean ever so slightly out of her booth.

"Yes, that's what I meant," he said with a strained grin.

"And you, sir?"

"I'll have the shepherd's pie," my dad ordered, "and

the green garlic and pea soup."

The waiter took our menus and scampered off to the kitchen as Alexander glared at me.

"What did you order, Dad?" I asked, horrified.

"Shepherd's pie."

"No—the soup."

"Green garlic. Why, would you like to order some? We can get the waiter."

All at once, I imagined the plate of green garlic and pea soup being placed within smelling distance of my vampire boyfriend. Alexander would wheeze; then he'd turn even more deathly pale than he already was. He'd stand up, staggering and gasping for air. We were miles away from the Mansion, Jameson, and Alexander's life-saving antidote.

"No—Alexander is deathly allergic to garlic!" I panicked. "We have to stop them; they can't bring it out!"

My dad's easygoing disposition turned to concern. He tossed his napkin on the table. "I'll cancel that immediately," he announced, and hurried off to find the waiter.

"I'm so sorry," my mother apologized. "Can he eat nuts?"

"Yes, it's just garlic he can't handle."

My dad returned to our table. "I changed it to a vegetable soup. You're not allergic to green beans, are you?" my dad teased.

We all laughed.

"That's an odd allergy," my dad said. "How long have you had that?"

"All my life. My whole family is allergic," Alexander said innocently. "They've always been."

"Ahem," I said, clearing my throat.

I was getting overheated. My face was starting to flush and my heart was throbbing. First of all I was out on a double date with my parents; secondly my date was a vampire; and thirdly at any moment between the stacks of *Abstract Algebra* and *Mathematics in Action*, my brother might be meeting up with a tween bloodsucker.

"Excuse me," I said, shooting my chair back, "I'll just be a moment."

Alexander rose politely, like a southern gentleman, as I rushed off to the ladies' room.

I was walking around the crowded bar when I bumped into someone.

"Excuse me," I apologized.

"Following me to restaurants now?" a familiar voice said. I looked up. My heartbeat screeched to a halt. It was Trevor.

"I believe I was here first."

"Technically not. I believe my mother was. I'm surprised to see you here. I thought you only ate in your dungeon," he said with a sneering grin.

Ever since Alexander and I had diverted Jagger and Luna from turning Trevor into a late-night snack at the Graveyard Gala—Trevor's party at Dullsville's cemetery—I'd gained a little respect from Trevor at school. Though my nemesis didn't know the Maxwells' true intent, he did know that for the last several days I had been warning him about the nefarious duo. Still, Trevor couldn't resist egging me on. His repartee was only slightly less biting than it used to be. Trevor and I'd been caustic to each other since kindergarten—it was the only way we knew how to communicate. Without that, we'd have no relationship. And that, I knew for sure, Trevor wasn't ready to give up.

"Is Alexander asking your father for your hand in marriage?"

"Don't be lame—"

"Not even to prom? It's next week. You'll miss watching me be crowned Prom King. Too bad they don't have a place for Prom Freak. They surely would have a tiara waiting for you."

I snarled at my nemesis and glanced over at Alexander, who was politely engaged in conversation with my parents.

Prom? I hadn't even thought about prom since Jagger, Luna, and now Valentine had arrived in town. Dullsville High was so small, all grades were invited to attend. Finally, I, Raven Madison, queen of the outcasts, had a potential date with the most gorgeous guy in all of Dullsville to the most important dance of the year, and I hadn't even had the time to daydream about it.

My best friend, Becky, was so busy with her boyfriend, Matt, that she and I hadn't had a chance to dish about the prom. Of course, she'd be attending the ball with Matt, and Trevor would arrive with some gorgeous blond varsity cheerleader. And I would be escorted by Alexander Sterling. But would he even go after the fiasco at the Snow Ball several months ago where Trevor challenged him, forcing him to retreat to the Mansion?

And would there even *be* a prom if the town of Dullsville knew that a preteen vampire was lurking somewhere in town?

"Don't forget to vote for me," my nemesis said, disappearing into the crowd of patrons.

I ducked into the ladies' room, washed my hands in the white porcelain sink, and reapplied bloodred eyeliner to the corners of my eyes and snow-colored powder to my nervous brow.

How would I manage to get us to the library in the middle of dinner with my parents, while the curious Mitchells sat at an adjacent table, without making a scene?

It would take a miracle—or at least a ghost white lie.

"I think Billy Boy should be with us," I said when I returned to our table.

My parents looked at me skeptically.

"He's at a Math Club party. I told you that," my mom reminded me. "They're providing dinner."

"You know how much he loves eating here. He's crazy about the Cricket burgers. Now I feel bad, eating at one of his favorite restaurants without him—"

"We can bring something home for him," my dad offered. "Why the sudden interest in your brother?"

Clearly my father wasn't making this easy.

"He loves the big-screen TVs. He whines enough as it is. I'll have to hear about it for weeks."

"You don't need your little brother as a buffer, do you?" my mom asked. "Paul, I think we're embarrassing her. We'll stop asking so many questions."

"No, you guys are great," I assured my parents. "I just think he'd be upset to know we were so close and didn't include him. How about Alexander and I just run over and pick him up?" I suggested. "It's only a few blocks away. We'll be back before our dinner arrives."

"He's having his own party," my dad said. "Right now they are probably exchanging prime numbers."

"Well, if that's what you really want, Paul," Mom said.

"All right, I'll get him," my dad said resignedly, putting his napkin on the table.

"No—I want to," I said, standing up before my father could. "Alexander's never been to the library."

My dad looked at me suspiciously. "Are you sure you're not sneaking off to a rave?"

"In this town? No, but if I find out about one, you'll know where we are," I said with a wink.

3

Dead Tree Forest

Alexander and I set off to do something I never thought I'd do: crash a Math Club party.

My vampire boyfriend held my hand as we hurried through the strip mall parking lot, across a two-lane side street, and around a gas station. We were briskly walking past the small wooded area next to the library when we heard something off in the distance. It was the sound of a dog howling.

We stopped in our tracks. Hair stood up on the back of my neck. The dog howled again.

Dead Tree Forest, as I called it, was a two-acre undeveloped property with thick brush and foliage surrounding an inner layer of decay. The trees reached out for the sun and rain in vain; all that remained were wooden skeletons. Sometimes on the weekends I'd get my research from the library and do my homework among the rotting oaks and maples. There were more dead trees than live ones, but the heavy brush made it difficult to see through to the streets once inside the woods.

In the seventies it was rumored that the woods were a haven for drunken motorcycle gangs. Others claimed no one was ever heard of coming out of the woods at nighttime alive.

Streetlights illuminated the darkened exterior, casting an eerie glow.

"Maybe Valentine is in there," I wondered aloud. "Can you see him?"

"I can see in the dark, but I don't have X-ray vision."

"Valentine could be searching for more than a tree house—perhaps a meal? What if he plans to pounce on my brother the moment he walks out of the library?"

The dog howled again.

Alexander looked at me as if he, too, was uncertain about what lay in the woods—or rather who.

"All right," he said valiantly, and proceeded toward the trees.

Now I was concerned for *us*. I clutched my boyfriend's arm.

"Wait," I warned. "Who knows what he'll do. Maybe we should just head for the library."

"You do realize he is eleven," Alexander said to me.

"But the same blood that runs through his veins also runs through Jagger's and Luna's. He isn't like any other eleven-year-old. Plus, you know better than I do what he is capable of."

"You're right," he agreed, putting his hand firmly on my shoulder. "That's why you are staying here. If I can talk to Valentine, we can put this whole thing to rest. I'll be right back."

Alexander pulled back a branch and disappeared into the brush.

I waited for a moment, my heart pounding with anxiety. I couldn't see anything from my vantage point. I wouldn't be hurting anyone if I poked my head in to get a better view.

I pulled a branch back and crept inside the thick brush.

The foliage blocked out much of the streetlight and I could barely see the skinny trees before me. I guided myself around them with an outstretched hand in the faint moonlight.

The wind whistled through the barren trees. I passed a creepy white broken fence with only a few pickets left, leaning like aging tombstones. I managed to carefully step over a few stumps, downed branches, and fallen trees.

I couldn't see Alexander anywhere. I could hardly make out the woodpiles, rocks, and discarded mattresses that were before me. Just then I heard a branch snap.

I spun around.

"Alexander?"

I didn't feel the familiar presence of my boyfriend. I turned back around and cautiously crept forward.

It was impossible to tell where I was. I studied the ground to see if I'd made tracks, but the hardened dirt and dead grass showed no signs of combat boots. I stepped once more, not knowing if I was going toward the street or farther into the woods.

The dog howled another time. Its cries seemed stronger. Was it howling at Valentine—or my own true love?

"Alexander—where are you?"

I remembered my parents were waiting for us at the Cricket Club. Alexander and I were supposed to return before the meals reached the table. We would have been back before the fish and chips arrived if I hadn't diverted us into the woods.

"Alexander!" I called again.

Then I realized if Valentine was here, my continued shouting was calling attention to my location.

I heard a fluttering in the trees above me. I could barely see what looked like two frightened squirrels racing up a branch, running away from a winged creature. It looked like a bird, but then the moonlight illuminated its small, mouselike face. This was no bird—it was a bat. It hovered in place intently, then headed straight for me.

I raised my arm to cover my face.

"Alexander!"

Nothing happened.

I opened my eyes and saw the creature fly overhead, through a break in the trees, into the night sky. Then it disappeared.

A hand fell hard on my shoulder.

I opened my mouth to speak, but no words came out. I turned around.

"I told you to stay outside on the sidewalk," my boyfriend scolded.

"Was that you?"

"Was what me?"

"That bat?"

"What bat?" Alexander plucked a few twigs out of my hair and shirt, which I now knew he could easily see in the dark, and grabbed my hand. "Let's get your brother," he instructed softly.

As Alexander led me back through the woods, I glanced up at the moon, wondering what, or maybe who, I'd just seen.

Dullsville's library was a freestanding two-story brick building with white colonial columns, built in the late nineteenth century.

My favorite memories of visiting the library were during Halloween. The librarians did their best to make it scary and fun. They'd decorate the shelves with cobwebs, dangle plastic spiders from computers, and place "terrorific" authors like Edgar Allan Poe, Stephen King, and Mary Shelley on display. I'd be greeted at the door by a witch and later check out a book from a werewolf.

However, today wasn't Halloween and I was going to be checking out more than literature. Alexander and I breezed through the automatic doors and past the "Used Books" drop box, the table of upcoming events, a cart of returned books, and the circular information desk.

We cased every aisle to see if Valentine might be

hiding behind one. The library was empty of its regular and visiting readers, but a few Math Club family members were biding their time surfing the Internet. Alexander and I searched the fiction aisles and then wandered through the DVD and CD section. A few siblings were hanging out in the teen section. Valentine wasn't around, and neither was Billy Boy.

A young woman with a checkered sweater and jeans was restocking books. "May I help you?" she inquired.

"Can you tell me where the Math Club is having their party?" I asked.

She pointed to the stairwell and adjacent elevator. "Lower level, behind children's literature, in the conference room."

As Alexander and I descended the aging staircase, I could smell the strange scent of old books combined with the intoxicating scent of cheese pizza.

When we reached the bottom, we saw a fountain with rocks running along the back wall. It held some hefty goldfish, and gold and silver coins lay at the bottom like sunken treasures. A woman was sitting with her child as the little girl innocently tried to pet the yellow swimmers.

"My mom brought me here when I was little. She used to give me a penny to throw into the fountain," I shared with Alexander as we walked past a round child-sized table riddled with picture books. "My wish was always the same. That I'd become a vampire." I gazed into his eyes. "Maybe that wish can finally come true."

Instead of answering, Alexander led me toward the conference room.

We walked by shelves of picture books, tables of computers, and posters of the Cat in the Hat, Curious George, and Babar. The normally quiet library was filled with the sounds of kids talking and laughing.

We finally reached the doors of the conference room. A long rectangular table was covered with pizza, popcorn, chips, and all the soda a preteen's bladder could hold.

A middle-aged man, who looked more like a football coach than a librarian in his sweatshirt and jeans, was at the head of the room, pulling a movie screen down over the blackboard.

About twenty kids in all were having a blast, hanging out on the weathered brown carpeting, lounging in beanbag and folding chairs, playing with MP3 players or Gameboys, and munching on snacks.

Stationed at the doorway, I quickly scanned the room, searching for any white-haired preteen. I breathed a sigh of relief when I didn't see Valentine. But I did see something I never thought I'd witness—my pesky sibling entertaining a small group of students who had gathered on the floor around him, cracking up like he was a nerdy Chris Rock.

I was stunned. I'd always called Billy "Nerd Boy" for a reason, but now he was shining in a way I'd never seen before. I realized the scrawny little brother that I'd always picked on my whole life had something I didn't have—a club of peers that he related to and who looked up to him as if he were a king.

I hated to admit it, but I felt a tinge of pride and a tiny bit of jealousy. My puny little brother was lucky to have a group to belong to—something I had never had. There was Chess Club, French Club, but never the Goth Club. I imagined a preteen roomful of students like Alexander and myself, eating gummy worms, reading Bram Stoker's *Dracula*, and watching *Queen of the Damned*.

Suddenly the laughter stopped, and the students glared at us, like we were the nerdy ones.

Billy Boy turned around. "What are you doing here?" he asked, joining Alexander and me by the door. "Is something wrong?"

"Have you seen that pasty kid with black fingernails that you promised to show Henry's treehouse to?"

"No. I told him we had Math Club tonight, so we agreed to meet at Henry's tomorrow at sunset. He eats dinner late," Billy Boy explained. "I thought maybe he might meet us here, but I haven't seen him. Why?"

"Never mind . . . Mom and Dad are waiting for us at the Cricket Club. We want you to come over."

"The Cricket Club," he said enthusiastically. "But I've already eaten."

"It doesn't matter; you can get dessert."

"But *Star Wars* is about to start. And I promised I'd go home with Henry."

Billy Boy was at the age where he preferred the company of his friends to his family. I nearly felt torn insisting my brother join us when he was having such a great time at the party, but I didn't have a choice. Valentine might be lurking in the Dead Tree Forest—or anywhere in Dullsville, for that matter.

"We'll bring Henry with us," I said sternly.

The preteen techno wizard then sauntered over. "Hi, guys. Have you come to watch the movie?"

"No, we've come to take you and my brother to dinner. We have to hurry; Mom and Dad are waiting."

The librarian came over. His generous smile couldn't mask his concern that my brother was talking to a dark stranger.

"This is my sister—and her boyfriend." Billy Boy introduced us with a hint of pride.

"We are just about to start the movie," the book man began. "You are welcome to stay."

"Henry and I will have to take a rain check," Billy Boy replied. "We have a match at the the Cricket Club."

Back at the restaurant, Alexander placed his hand on my knee in between bites of his "bloody" steak. The Mitchells continued to eyeball us as Billy Boy and Henry took over the conversation, talking about computer math and the strange boy they met a few days ago at the library.

"Maybe you shouldn't invite a boy over you don't know," my mother said, sounding worried.

"That's what I said."

"Did he transfer to your school?" she questioned.

"No, I think he's visiting," Billy Boy replied.

"Who?" my mom asked. "Do you know his family?"

Billy Boy turned to Henry, who just shrugged his shoulders.

"I'm not sure I like you hanging around a boy who

nobody knows anything about."

The truth was, Alexander and I *did* know—we just couldn't tell.

"Well, we'll find out all about him when we meet him tomorrow," Billy Boy concluded.

My dad quickly changed the conversation to Billy Boy's upcoming English project.

"It's Facts Versus Folklore. We got to choose from a bunch of myths and legends—mermaids, werewolves, trolls. Henry and I picked vampires. I figured if we bring in Raven we'll get an easy A," my brother said with a laugh.

"Billy—be kind," my mother scolded.

Little did they know who the real vampire at the table was.

In spite of my family's intense inquiries, I could see Alexander was having fun. I felt a twinge of melancholy for my beloved, who'd been forced to leave Romania and his family. I wondered if I would have been able to leave my whole family and Becky behind, move to another country, and live in a lonely old Mansion with just a butler for company. Even though the creepy man himself, Jameson, was a dear and trusted friend to Alexander and the Sterling family, he was centuries older. I'm sure the odd couple didn't talk about music, girls, and movies.

Alexander never once complained. However, I was relieved that I'd snuck into the Mansion and found my Goth mate there. By the way my boyfriend was beaming here at the Cricket Club, I'm sure he felt the same way.

Now that we all were together, I knew my family and I were safe. I just didn't know for how long.

After dropping Henry off, we all arrived home, our bellies filled with vinegar and chips and chocolate ice cream.

"I appreciate your inviting me out to dinner," Alexander said to my parents.

"We'll have to do it again," my dad said, shaking Alexander's hand.

I walked my boyfriend to Jameson's car.

"Tomorrow we'll have to be at the treehouse at sunset," he said to me as he leaned against the Mercedes.

Alexander touched my cheek with the back of his pale hand, then cupped my chin. He leaned in to give me a lingering good-night kiss.

I watched him as he drove down the street, off to his attic room. He would make the night pass with music and art until it was time to return to his coffin.

I opened my own bedroom door to find my kitten, Nightmare, on my bookshelf, hissing. I was holding her in my arms, softly stroking her nose, when I heard a scream. It came from Billy Boy's room.

I had just released Nightmare onto my bed and raced into the hallway when Billy Boy flew out of his room, crashing into me.

He almost knocked the wind out of me. "Get off, you doofus!" I yelled. "What's wrong with you?"

Billy Boy didn't speak; instead he pointed into his room. His door remained partially closed. It creaked as I slowly pushed it open.

The way he had screamed, I expected to see a dead body.

Nothing looked out of place—his dresser, closet, and bed were all in order.

"What's wrong with you? You were screaming like a girl!"

He shook his head and kept pointing in the direction of his computer desk. "Over there."

I crept over and glanced around. "Yes, this would frighten me, too," I said, holding up a pre-algebra book. "You are only in the fifth grade."

"No, outside—"

I peered out into the backyard. I could see our swing set and my dad retrieving a garden hose. I stepped back. Then out of the corner of my eye, I saw something move. Hanging upside down from the window casing was a very live bat. Two beady green eyes pierced through me. I couldn't move.

Just then my mom appeared. "I was in the basement and I heard someone shouting."

I turned to see Billy Boy poking his head out from behind my mother.

I looked back toward the window. The bat was gone.

"What happened?" my mom wondered aloud.

"Nothing," I said. "I think Billy Boy is afraid of his shadow."

"It was a bat!" he protested. "It had green eyes."

"Bats don't have green eyes," my mother argued.

"This one did and it was staring right at me!" my brother urged.

"It must be all that Mountain Dew you drank," I began, "combined with that Cricket Club hot fudge sundae. It all rushed to your head."

"Let's calm down," my mother ordered. "You both need some rest before school."

My mother went over to the window and peered out. She shrugged her shoulders and pulled his curtains closed. Then she switched off his computer desk lamp. "All the shadows are gone."

Billy Boy cornered me at the door as my mom went back downstairs. "I know you saw it," he said. "Just 'cause you didn't tell her doesn't mean you can catch it. It's not going to be your new pet."

"Don't worry. I couldn't afford to feed it," I said truthfully, and pushed my way past him.

That night I was more restless than usual. Not only had dozing off in Alexander's coffin disrupted my sleep pattern, but I was exhilarated. I, Raven Madison, had spent the daylight snuggling in a coffin with my vampire boyfriend. I wanted to scream it from the top of my lungs! I went to the window and peered out into the darkness. I didn't want to be alone.

I'd give anything to spend an eternity with Alexander in his attic room, in our cozy coffin. But there would be a price. I would have to say good-bye to all that I knew and loved—my parents, my best friend, Becky, even Billy Boy.

And then I would be trading mortal nemeses for nocturnal ones. I wondered if being a vampiress would bring me any closer to the Maxwells. In the underworld, except for Alexander, I might find myself even lonelier than in Dullsville.

I lay in bed, Nightmare cuddling at my feet while I doodled sketches of Valentine in my Olivia Outcast journal. He was a cartoonish-looking kid with spiky white hair, tattoos, and piercings.

Above him, I drew a bat with green eyes. I thought about where an eleven-year-old vampire could be sleeping his daylight hours away—Dullsville's cemetery? The attic of an old church? Or maybe he was hiding in piles of leaves in the Oakley Woods. And I wondered what he might be doing alone in Dullsville at night—spying on tween mortals, searching for vacant treehouses, or marking his future unsuspecting Dullsvillian prey? But then I began to think about how Valentine must be lonely without his family, isolated from his friends or guardians. Did he run away from home? Why wasn't Valentine with Jagger and Luna?

Then I drew Jagger—his blue and green hypnotic eyes, his skull tattoo, his white hair with bloodred-tipped ends. Above him, I sketched a bat with piercing blue and green eyes. I wondered what Jagger really wanted in life. Was he back home in Romania biting the necks of teenagers out for a night of clubbing? Did he really crave to be a soccer star, as Luna had revealed to me, the same way he craved blood?

I drew an image of Luna. A gothic fairy princess with long white hair and baby-doll blue eyes, decked out in a tight black dress with pink rubber bracelets, a choker, and pink combat boots. Above her I drew a bat with ocean blue eyes. A kindred spirit of sorts. I imagined her back in Romania, thrashing it up at an underground club, the flashing lights twinkling against her like tiny ghosts as she danced the night away, oblivious to the handsome clubsters surrounding her, and waiting for the perfect moment to stop and pick the neck she wanted to taste.

Not only was she bonded to her brother Jagger, but someday she'd be bonded to another vampire for all of eternity.

Luna had actually accepted me as a vampiress. She complimented me on my style instead of being repulsed by it.

But our relationship was really built on lies. I had convinced her I was from the Underworld, and she had fooled me into thinking she desired Trevor when in fact it was Alexander she wanted all along.

I guess in our deceit we deserved each other.

I'm sure Alexander could paint the teen and tween vampires as precisely as a photograph, but I managed to capture their essence. The images stared back at me as if they were real. I closed my journal on the rendered Maxwells and looked forward to tomorrow, when Alexander and I might finally put an end to their invasion of Dullsville.

The next morning, Dullsville High's hallways were dec-
orated with posters for the upcoming prom. VIVA LAS
VALENTINES signs with red, pink, and white hearts filled
the walls and classroom doorways.

I shoved textbooks into my locker as Becky began to
tack up passport-sized arcade booth pictures of her and
Matt.

"We took these Saturday night at the movie theater.
Aren't they cool?"

I stared at the four poses—one with Matt's arm
around Becky, one with them blinking, one where he was
kissing her on the cheek, and the last with a *Teen* magazine
smile—all of them reflecting a couple in love.

I gazed at my locker—tacked with magazine clippings
of Trent Reznor, Marilyn Manson, Ville Valo . . . and
vacant of the one guy who meant the most to me.

"I figured by now you'd have a shrine to Alexander," Becky commented.

"I did, too," I admitted. *That was before I knew he was a vampire,* I wanted to say. "He's actually quite shy around the camera."

"No way. He's so handsome, he could be a model."

I glanced at my best friend, whose normally cherubic fresh face glowed more than ever. Always quiet and mousy, she was gaining confidence now that she'd been dating Matt.

I'd always blabbed my secrets to Becky. I was bursting to tell her the truth about Alexander—why I didn't have a picture shrine, why Alexander didn't attend Dullsville High, and why he was seen only at night. Carrying this secret around was a heavier burden than a backpack full of textbooks.

Becky was so happy with her boyfriend—taking pictures together, renting movies, watching him play soccer. I'd always craved more—to fly, to live in the darkness, to be eternally bonded to my soul mate. But at that moment, I realized I wanted to be like any girl who was lucky enough to be in love and hang her boyfriend's picture in her locker.

"Do you have your prom dress?" Becky asked, bringing me back to reality.

"Uh . . . well . . ."

"I can't believe it. We have dates to prom!"

"Yeah . . ."

"Aren't you going?" she asked, confused.

"It's just that . . ."

"You haven't asked Alexander yet?" she guessed. "It's next weekend."

"Of course I asked him," I stumbled. "He said he wouldn't miss it for the world."

She smiled with relief. "Yesterday, my mother and I picked out a dress and put it on hold. We're picking it up after school. Want to come?"

"I'd love to, but I have to meet Alexander and my brother. It's a long story. . . ."

"Oh, that's okay," she said, trying to cover up her disappointment. "Perhaps another time."

"But I can't wait to see your dress. I know you'll look fabulous in it."

She beamed like I'd told her she won a beauty pageant. "What does your dress look like," she asked, "besides black?"

"Dress? Oh, yeah. I guess I'll have to get one," I said, just as first bell rang. "But where in Dullsville am I going to find a dress?"

Alexander and I arrived at Henry's house to find his backyard vacant of any preteens, vampire or otherwise.

"Hurry, let's check the treehouse before my brother and Henry show up."

We walked past the pool, lounge chairs, and gazebo, which were illuminated by the backyard house lights, and crept into the shadows where the treehouse was.

I hung on to Alexander's silver bullet belt and followed him through the darkness. I remained at the foot of the tree as Alexander combed the grass and brush.

"Wait here," he said, reaching for the ladder.

I folded my arms like a toddler. "You mean you're going to leave me here alone?"

Alexander shook his head. "Good point. Stay close and be careful."

He extended his hand and guided me as I took my first step up the ladder in the darkness.

Alexander followed closely behind me. When we reached the deck, I headed for the treehouse door, only to find as many locks on it as a New York apartment.

"Maybe there's a chimney I can climb down," I said, frustrated.

Alexander attempted to jimmy the door. I tried to peek inside the windows, but the curtains were drawn.

"It'll just take me a second," he said confidently. "Then I'll open the door for you from inside," Alexander suggested.

Suddenly we heard the sound of the nerd-mates coming from Henry's poolside.

"We'll have to wait now," Alexander instructed. He leaned on the treehouse railing, staring out into the backyard, while I mustered up enough courage to bring up the one thing I'd repressed since he'd picked me up.

I didn't have much time. The nerd-mates' voices were getting closer.

"I have to ask you something . . . ," I began.

"Yes?" He gazed at me with his melting chocolate eyes, his silky black hair flopping in his face.

I took a deep breath. I had no problem searching for

ghosts or picnicking in a graveyard, but when it came to laying out my heart, my bravado ceased. And even though Alexander and I'd been dating for a few months, I felt I had more to lose than if I'd just met him.

"It's something I know you'll think is totally lame. Especially after we already went to the Snow Ball and that was a disaster."

"Don't say that. I got to dance with you."

The only good memory of that night was Alexander and me clubbing it up in Dullsville's gymnasium—plastic icicles and snowflakes hanging from the ceiling, fake powdery snow covering the floor, while artificial snow softly sprinkled down from the rafters.

"So what do you want to ask me?" he continued.

"I want to know . . ."

"Yes?"

"If you'll go with me . . ."

"Spit it out."

". . . to prom."

Alexander paused, his brow furrowed. Then he brushed his flopping hair away from his face. His silence was punctuated by chirping crickets. It seemed like they were waiting for his answer as much as I was. "But you're only a sophomore," he stated, confused.

I'd fantasized about him responding yes, I'd imagined him saying no. I didn't envision this.

"Everyone in high school can attend," I told him. "Lucky me. Instead of not being asked for two years, I can not be asked for four."

"No one invited you?" he asked, shocked, then clearly

relieved. "Good, because if some dude stole you away," he said with a grin, "I'd have way more bite than Jagger and Valentine combined."

I shook my head. "You don't want to go, just say it!" I turned away from him.

Alexander gently pulled me back toward him. "I thought I'd said yes."

"But you didn't." I frowned.

"Raven, I wouldn't miss it for the world."

My heart melted. "That's what I told Becky you'd say!"

I reached my arms out and gave him a huge hug. He picked me up, swung me around, and gave me a long kiss.

"Gross!" Billy Boy exclaimed, appearing on the tree-house deck. "What are you two doing here?"

Alexander released me from our embrace. I straightened out my shirt, flipped my hair back off my shoulder, and wiped my black lips.

"Have you seen Valentine?" I asked.

"No, he should be here by now," Billy Boy replied. "I don't mean to be rude, but this is not a love fest. New rules . . . This treehouse is for guys only. No girls allowed."

"Henry, can you unlock the locks?" I asked, ignoring my brother's remarks.

"So you can make out?" my brother sneered.

"No, creep. I want to show Alexander the stellar view."

"Man, everyone is interested in your treehouse," Billy said, crossing his arms. "Maybe you should sell tickets."

"You're right," Henry said. "Of course I'll let you in, but it'll cost you."

"Cost me?" I scoffed.

"I get ten percent," Billy Boy chimed in. "After all, it was my idea."

"Five bucks," Henry said firmly.

"Five dollars! You'll pay *me* five dollars for not kicking your—," I said, lunging toward the nerd-mates.

"Here," Alexander interrupted, grabbing my arm with one hand and reaching in his back pocket with the other. He pulled out his wallet and handed Henry a ten-dollar bill.

Henry inspected the money as if he were looking for drying ink.

"It's real," I said. "Give us the keys."

Henry pulled out his cell phone and intensely pressed a seven-digit number.

Alexander and I glanced at each other curiously.

We heard a ringing coming from the doorknob. The locks popped and the door creaked partially open.

Henry stood proudly gazing at his handmade gadgetry.

I started for the door, but the nerd-mates followed me.

"You guys wait here," I ordered. "You didn't buy tickets, we did."

"It's Henry's treehouse."

Alexander reached into his wallet and pulled out a five. "This should cover a private tour."

Henry quickly put the money into his chinos pocket. "No kissing, disrobing, or touching anything besides the telescope," he ordered. "I just assembled it."

I rolled my eyes.

"We'll be standing outside the door," Billy Boy warned.

I tiptoed inside, Alexander following closely behind me.

The folding tables were still lined with beakers and petri dishes. Henry's telescope was standing next to the front window. The black curtain, separating the treehouse into two rooms, was closed. The first time I'd pulled the curtain back, I'd found Jagger's stickered coffin and Luna's pink one. Those had been removed when Alexander and I inspected it a few days after the Graveyard Gala. This time, I wasn't sure what I would find.

I took a deep breath and yanked back the curtain.

I found an empty room.

What was he searching for?

There must be something lurking inside the treehouse that we didn't discover when we'd come to see that Jagger and Luna had gone.

"I guess Valentine's not staying here," I said.

"Maybe he plans to," Alexander suspected.

In the corner, a small closet door was slightly ajar. I reached inside and found a cardboard box hidden in the shadows. Perhaps it was the candelabra, pewter goblet, or Luna's gothic makeup. Or more likely jars of molds and spores to be examined under Henry's microscope. I peered inside and noticed rolled-up parchment paper.

I unwound the rubber band and quickly unrolled them. It was a stack of graveyard etchings, like the ones Jagger collected from graveyards he'd been to and used as grim artwork to decorate the treehouse, the abandoned mill, and his apartment at the Coffin Club.

"Jagger must have left these behind," I concluded.

"Time's up!" I heard my brother call.

I didn't even have time to read the etchings. I rolled them back up, rewound the rubber band, and stuck the papers underneath my shirt.

I pulled back the curtain and found Henry and Billy Boy glaring at us like Alexander and I were in trouble.

"What's that?" Henry asked in an accusatory tone.

"What's what?" I asked, faking shock.

"Stuck under your shirt," Henry accused.

Reluctantly, I pulled the rolls out. "You mean this? Just a scrap of paper."

"Those are my maps of constellations!" He extended his hand. I had no choice but to give him back his papers, even though they weren't maps. Henry pulled back the curtain and placed the rolled-up etchings in a small closet and locked the door.

At that moment, we all heard a group of dogs barking off in the distance.

Suddenly a chill was in the air. Alexander seemed distracted.

He stepped out onto the treehouse deck.

I pointed the telescope toward the front window and peered through. The image of Henry's street was blurry, but I could just make out a white-haired boy staring straight at me.

I gasped and quickly pulled the image into focus. The boy, a miniature version of Jagger in a white T-shirt and oversized black shorts, was speeding away down the street on a coffin-shaped skateboard.

6

Gothic's Orders

S tay away from Valentine," I commanded to Billy Boy
when we walked through our front door. "He's
trouble."

Billy Boy rolled his eyes. "Just because he didn't show?
Something must have come up," he surmised. "Besides,
I'm sure he's just lonely. I've never seen him at school, so
he probably needs a friend," he said, stopping at the foot
of the stairs.

"It doesn't matter; you have a friend already."

"You're not my boss."

"Running around with him can lead to all sorts of
mess."

"How do you know? You don't even know him."

"I can just tell."

"Why, because he has tattoos and wears black? You're
judging Valentine, just like everyone judges you. Just

because he has black fingernails doesn't mean he's a monster—that's how you've defended yourself for years. And now look at you, behaving just like the town reacts to you."

Billy Boy would've had a point if Valentine wasn't a vampire.

Even so, maybe my brother was right. Maybe Valentine was more like Alexander than Jagger. Maybe I was making assumptions that weren't fair.

"The day you start listening to others is the day I start listening to you," he said, and stormed up the stairs to his room.

"What's going on?" my mom asked as I entered the kitchen to find her wiping off the countertop. "I heard you two shouting."

"Nothing," I replied, opening the refrigerator.

"One minute you're insisting we include your brother at dinner, the next you're yelling at each other."

"I thought that was normal," I said, grabbing a soda.

"I guess it is . . . ," she admitted.

I closed the refrigerator door. "I have some news," I said. "I'm going to prom."

My mother's face lit up as if I were a twenty-five-year-old woman announcing my engagement.

"Congratulations!" she exclaimed, hugging me hard. "We'll have to buy you a dress and shoes."

"That's not necessary," I said, twisting off the plastic bottlecap. "I'll find something at the thrift store."

My mother wrinkled her nose. "You'll be attending

prom, not a nightclub. We'll get you something beautiful to wear that isn't torn, adorned with staples, or riddled with safety pins."

That's exactly what I was afraid of.

I'd finally seen Valentine—even if it was only for a moment through a telescope. As I tried to finish my language arts essay, my mind was distracted by the eleven-year-old vampire. I imagined what he wanted at the tree-house—a hidden treasure, Jagger's leftover blood supply, a place to lay his coffin? I also envisioned all the places he could be speeding off to on his skateboard—Dullsville's cemetery, a hidden sewer, or an abandoned church. And most important, I wondered when I'd see him again.

7

Shopghoul

The next day, after the second bell before language arts class, Becky was reviewing her completed essay, while I was trying to keep my weary eyes open long enough to finish mine. Our teacher, Mr. Kensy, a dour man with a devilish mustache, was taking attendance when the announcements came on.

"Viva las Valentines," a perky teen girl's voice began over the classroom loudspeaker. "Prom is just around the corner. Don't forget to purchase tickets at the gymnasium door during lunch period. Also cast your ballots for Prom King and Queen. His and Her Majesty will get a spotlight dance and a picture in the *Chatterbox*."

Our class treasurer, a blond with a bob, wearing a pink-and-white-striped polo shirt and jeans, rose and shyly walked down the classroom aisles, handing a red valentine to each student.

Becky began to scribble pensively, as if she were voting in her first presidential election.

As the other students whispered and wrote down their choices, I quickly filled out my form.

"I'll show you mine if you show me yours," I said to Becky when I'd finished.

Becky nodded eagerly.

I held out my valentine—next to King I'd written "Matt Wells," and next to Queen I'd written "Becky Miller." A huge smile lit up my best friend's face.

Becky showed me her ballot. Next to King she'd written with perfect penmanship "Alexander Sterling." Next to Queen it read "Raven Madison."

"I like the sound of it," I announced. "But Alexander doesn't attend our school."

We folded our ballots and as the treasurer walked back up the row we stuck them in a homemade aluminum-foil-covered box resembling something children make in elementary school.

"We each got one vote," I said proudly. "Now we just need three hundred ninety-nine more!"

My mom was so overjoyed that I'd be attending prom, she ducked out of work early, picked me up from school in her SUV, and drove me to Jack's department store.

Jack's department store was originally owned by Jack Patterson's father and was now run by Jack, a handsome crush-worthy guy five years my senior. When I was twelve, I'd snuck into the Mansion for him so he could pass an initiation for his high school buddies. He remembered me ever since and always wore a smile for me when I visited the department store.

Jack's sold everything from socks to scooters, Fiestaware to Waterford crystal, and generic wallets to Prada purses.

My mom and I entered the store, breezing past the linen department. Designer towels in every color on an artist's palette were neatly stacked on white shelves.

Focused on a fashion mission, my mom headed straight for the escalators.

"Juniors are on this floor," I instructed, pointing past Bedding.

"We're going to Juniors Boutique," she said.

I'd hardly been in the Juniors, much less Juniors Boutique. We rode the ascending escalator, peering down on shoppers perusing fine jewelry.

We reached the second floor, walked past Designer Women's Petites, and arrived at Juniors Boutique. Cashmere sweaters, designer blouses, and jeans were perfectly displayed. Anorexic mannequins flaunted size zero skirts and hundred-dollar tank tops.

About a dozen or so girls and their mothers were picking through the rows of dresses—pink, purple, violet, gray, red, green, lavender, black, some with rhinestones or lace, plunging necklines or conservative ones, sleeveless or strapless, floor-length or knee-length hems.

Each daughter was a Xerox copy of her mom. Except for our brunette hair, which my mother regularly colored, my mom and I appeared to be polar opposites.

One by one, my mother pulled dresses off the racks until she had two armfuls. One by one, I glanced over dresses and moved to another rack, empty-handed.

A seasoned sales manager, wearing a name tag that read MADGE and exuding the confidence of a sea captain effortlessly managing a vessel on the high seas, approached my mom.

"Here, let me take those," she said. This obviously wasn't her first prom season and it wasn't going to be her last. "I'll start a dressing room for you."

We followed the woman into the dressing room already flooded with prom babes strutting their gowns like they were on a Paris catwalk.

I disrobed, taking off my wide-bottom black jeans and Hello Batty T-shirt, and stepped into a pink satin number.

I stared into the full-length mirror. I didn't even recognize my own reflection.

"Let me see!" I heard my mother say.

Reluctantly, I opened the dressing-room door.

"Take off those boots!" she scolded. "This isn't a heavy metal concert."

As I untied my laces, Madge appeared and within moments she was back with pink rhinestone stilettos, size seven.

I stepped before the three-way dressing-room mirror.

I felt like a bridesmaid, but to my mother, I must have looked like the bride.

"You are beautiful!" she gushed.

Even Madge agreed. "You look like a model," she declared, and waited for my reaction.

I could see myself reflected in my mother's eyes, slowly transforming into the daughter she had always wanted.

The prom babes sized me up. A few smiled; a few giggled. I must have looked quite the sight, pretty in pink with my multiple ear piercings, temporary bat tattoos, and black lipstick and fingernail polish.

I imagined how much better I'd look if this prom dress had a few holes, black seams, or was dyed bloodred.

"Before you decide . . . ," Madge declared briskly. She returned to the counter to replace my black rubber bracelets with rhinestone ones.

Just then Jack Patterson stepped into view.

"Raven, it's Jack," my mother said, and excitedly exited the dressing room.

As my mother greeted Jack and they continued on with their pleasantries, I raced back to my dressing-room stall and locked the door.

Then she did something only a mother would do. "Raven! Come out here," she called to me.

I had nowhere to run. I wasn't ready for anyone to see me like this, much less Jack Patterson.

I slunk out of the dressing room, through Juniors Boutique, trying to balance myself on the tiny stiletto heels.

The other girls scrutinized me as they continued to shop. My mother signaled for me to twirl around and model the dress for Jack. I awkwardly spun like an inexperienced model.

Jack smiled. "You look beautiful."

I couldn't help but feel proud, even though I felt like an ornament on top of a sweet sixteen birthday cake.

"I have more to try on . . . ," I finally said, heading back to the dressing room.

After I tried on a dress in every color of the rainbow, the Madison mother-and-daughter Prom Dress Finding Team were growing weary.

I got dressed in my black-on-black threads.

"So which one do you like?" my mom asked, holding up a pink dress in one hand and a blue one in the other. "I think they are both wonderful."

"Uh . . . can we keep looking?"

I just imagined Alexander, sporting a midnight black tux, arriving at my house to find me all puffed up in pink.

"Why are you frowning?" my mother chided.

"They may be wonderful. . . . But they're not . . . me."

My mother sighed. "For my senior prom, Grandma bought me what she wanted me to wear—a lavender satin dress with a white sweater and brand-new crisp white gloves."

"Gloves? But you were a hippie."

"Exactly."

"So you wore them?"

"I did until I got to the prom. Then I switched into a sundress I had hanging in my locker. Now I'm doing the same thing to you. Insisting you dress the way I'd like you to dress instead of the way that makes you comfortable."

I was impressed that my mother had such insight. "Let's give it one more try," she continued.

There was a simple black strapless dress, lined with lace, on a mannequin. I could accessorize it with an onyx choker, black studded bracelets, and spiderweb earrings.

Jennifer Warren, a varsity cheerleader, stood behind me as I studied the dress, glaring at me as if I wasn't worthy of eyeing such a beautiful gown.

"Hey, Mom," I called, catching up to her at the accessory counter. "I think I've found a dress that fits both our tastes."

I led my mother back through the maze of satiny garments.

We reached the mannequin, only to find a salesgirl unzipping the black dress and handing it to Jennifer.

"Mom," Jennifer exclaimed to a delighted woman. "It's stunning."

My heart sank. I tugged at my hair and dug my boots into the masonite tiled floor. My eyes couldn't help but well up with tears. My mother's smile strained, as if she were as heartbroken as I was.

"That's fine," I managed to say. "I don't have to go."

"What do you mean you're not going?" Jack asked from behind the sales counter.

"They just sold the perfect dress," I admitted.

"You mean you didn't like the pink one?" he asked, helping a salesgirl with the register. "It looked gorgeous."

"Well . . ."

"Not your taste . . . I understand."

Jack thought for a moment as he finished the transaction. "Why don't you come with me . . ."

Jack motioned us behind the sales counter and we followed him down a hallway. "A few gowns just arrived this afternoon. It's been so busy, we haven't even had the chance to put them on the floor," he whispered. He unlocked a storeroom and led us through boxes of merchandise and hanging layaways to a rack of fancy junior dresses. "Take your time. If you are interested in anything, bring it to the sales desk."

"What are these?" I asked, pointing to a rack of costumes.

"Inventory from Halloween," he answered, heading for the door.

"Halloween?" my mother asked, horrified. "You're going to prom, not a Monster Mash."

"Please. Let me see!" I said, pushing past a rack of men's suits. "Thank you, Jack!"

"Yes, Jack. Thank you for all your help," my mother added.

I was as happy as a bat in a dusty old attic.

I rummaged through the hanging costumes—a fairy costume, a firefighter uniform, and a mermaid outfit.

"This is cool," I said, holding up a red devil dress.

"Absolutely not!" my mother said.

I frowned and returned it to the rack.

"This is not what I had in mind when I said let's buy a dress for prom. Shopping in a storeroom," she said, continuing her search. "However . . . take a look at this one."

I didn't even notice what my mom was holding up.

At the end of the rack, I saw a blood red skirt with black lace calling my name. I pulled the dress out and gasped.

On a hanger hung a dark red corset with black lace, black strings, and a matching ankle-length skirt.

Attached to the hanger was the most fabulous accessory I'd ever seen: a gloomy parasol.

"I love it!" I exclaimed, showing it to my mother. "It's not torn, and it doesn't have staples or safety pins."

My mother paused. "It's not really what I had in mind . . ."

I modeled it over my clothes and danced around.

"I wanted you to look like a modern-day princess, not a Victorian vampire."

"Isn't it wonderful?"

I gave my mother a huge squeeze.

Madge had sold hundreds of dresses in her time at Jack's, but by the way she forced her smile, I don't think she'd ever rung up a Halloween outfit for prom. However, the old woman did her best to mask her shock and dismay. "You can be confident that no one else will be wearing this dress," she proclaimed.

Between my mother and me, we finally compromised on a dress that suited her budget and wasn't one I'd have to change out of as soon as I got to prom.

* * *

That evening, Alexander was waiting for me outside the Mansion door, the serpent knocker eyeing me like an old friend. My vampire boyfriend was sporting tight black drill jeans with black buckles running down the side, a *Crow* T-shirt, and his backpack slung over one shoulder. He gave me a sweet hello kiss.

"Are we going back to the treehouse? Or going camping?" I asked coyly.

"Last night I returned to the treehouse to retrieve Jagger's gravestone etchings. They were gone."

"Valentine?" I asked.

"I assume so. Valentine won't be back to the treehouse for a while. It would be too risky for him."

"Then how will we ever find him?"

"We'll have to lead him to us. Remember the box of blood-filled amulets that Jagger received from the Coffin Club that I found in the cemetery? Jagger used them to sustain himself so he'd go unnoticed here in Dullsville. I've got some in here," Alexander said, patting his backpack. "We can leave a few for Valentine at a couple locations. That way we can tell where he's been."

We tied several amulets to one of the limbs of the treehouse before heading off in the Mercedes to Dullsville's cemetery.

"Valentine has to be hiding out somewhere," Alexander stated as he parked the car beside the cemetery.

Alexander held my hand as we headed up the sidewalk to the graveyard's entrance.

"I shouldn't be on sacred ground, should I?" I asked when we reached the iron gates. "If he did bite me, not only would he turn me into a vampire, but I'd be bonded to him for eternity."

Alexander paused.

"I guess you're right," he agreed. "I forget that Valentine is a . . . It's best you stay behind."

"Stay behind?" I asked with a puppy dog face, quickly changing my tune. "But Valentine isn't here to bond with a mate, is he?"

Alexander shook his head. "I'm not sure why he's here." My boyfriend started over the fence.

"But if Valentine isn't after an eternal partner, it couldn't hurt," I said, pulling myself over the fence.

I followed Alexander through the aisles of tombstones, past the caretaker's shed. We checked out a freshly dug grave.

"Nothing here," he declared as we looked into the empty grave. We reached the sycamore where we originally found the box of amulets.

Alexander placed five amulets on the ground—haphazardly, so they wouldn't appear to be a trap. "We'll wait for a few minutes."

We snuck behind the caretaker's shed. Alexander put his arm around me and we huddled together underneath the glow of the moonlight.

"Tell me about your day. I feel there is so much in your life that I am missing," Alexander began.

"Biology? Or algebra? You aren't missing a thing."

"I imagine you doodling in your notebooks, skipping class, eating with Matt and Becky."

"What do I look like?"

"Beautiful, like a dark angel glowing in the daylight that streams into the classroom. Like the picture of you I have beside my coffin."

I sighed. "Becky put up some photos in her locker yesterday that she and Matt had taken in a photo booth. I wish I had a picture of you."

Alexander gazed at me, his dark eyes sad.

"There are certain things I can never give you," he admitted, "that other guys at your school can."

"You give me so much more than any mortal can," I said reassuringly.

Alexander squeezed my hand. I could tell he felt lonely and wanted to join my world as much as I wanted to join his.

"It's getting late," he said.

"If we leave now, we may miss Valentine," I complained.

"I have a feeling he won't be back for a while. We can return tomorrow, together."

That night I was modeling my corseted prom dress in my bedroom and trying to match accessories from my Mickey Malice jewelry box. I put my onyx choker on and gazed into the mirror. I wondered how Alexander would prepare for prom without being able to see his reflection. Would I give up seeing my reflection forever to have the chance to be with Alexander for eternity? I wasn't sure how I'd adapt to not performing the tasks I'd grown accustomed to doing for the past sixteen years. If Dullsvillians thought I was a freak now, I'm sure they would have a field day when I applied my lipstick and eyeliner without the use of a mirror.

The following day Matt, Becky, and I met at our lockers, then headed to the gymnasium to purchase prom tickets. We squeezed through the claustrophobically crowded bustling hallways, past the main entrance, and turned the corner to the gym. There I saw something I'd never imagined—a huge line of kids snaking through the hall like the Loch Ness monster.

"Are they selling Rolling Stones tickets, too?" I joked.

"If so, I'm buying," Matt replied as we joined the end of the line. Every Dullsville High student must have been attending the upcoming prom. Some couples were holding hands, a few girls were on cell phones, another pair was having a fight. Matt put his arm around Becky and her face lit up like the New Year's Eve crystal ball at Times Square. I felt a pang in my heart because Alexander wasn't here to put his arm around me.

From my vantage point, I could barely see the entrance to the gym where several student ticket sellers were seated behind a folding table. Fortunately, the line seemed to be moving steadily along toward the destination. Our class treasurer was off to the side holding a clipboard like she was taking a survey.

"Sign-up sheet for volunteers. We need extra hands for the decorations," she said as we proceeded forward.

Becky waved over the girl in charge of our sophomore funds.

"Are you going to sign up?" Becky asked me as she scribbled her name on the paper.

"I don't have much free time these days."

When Becky was finished, the treasurer glared at me, quickly withdrew her clipboard before I had the chance to change my mind, and moved to the end of the line.

"Have you heard about a creepy-looking kid hanging out in town?" I overheard a couple say behind me as we moved a few feet ahead.

I angled my head slightly to get an earful. "Yes," the other answered. "I think he's related to those freaks from Romania that were at Trevor's Graveyard Gala. Supposedly he wanders the streets at night looking for souls."

I leaned back a little farther.

"I heard he was a ghost," the guy gossiped.

"Apparently the caretaker has been finding empty candy wrappers in the cemetery—"

"He wears that nasty *goth* clothing," she whispered, loud enough for me to hear.

I continued to lean back—this time a little too far. I lost my balance and stumbled back.

"Ouch," Heather Ryan complained. "That was my foot."

"Sorry," I said genuinely as I regained my footing.

If I had been a prep like her, she probably would have

laughed it off. But instead she looked at me as if I, too, had just climbed out of the cemetery looking for souls. "These are brand-new Pradas," she whined.

"Well, these are vintage Doc Martens. What's the big deal?"

"I think you may have scuffed them," she said, scowling at me.

I stared at her bright white shoes.

"You should be thanking me. I'd be glad to scuff them some more, if you like."

Her boyfriend laughed.

"It's not nice to eavesdrop," she reprimanded me as if she were a teacher.

"It's even worse to gossip," I snarled. "And very tacky to designer-name drop." We were fast approaching the ticket table. "You still have time to ask someone else," I whispered to her boyfriend.

He laughed again and she slugged him in the arm.

"Come on, Raven," Becky ordered, pulling me away. "It's our turn."

I left the gossipmongers and approached the ticket table.

Becky beamed as Matt bought two tickets.

I pulled out a wad of cash from my Olivia Outcast purse.

"No cutting," I heard the couple say in back of me. I turned around. Trevor Mitchell was standing behind me.

"So have you found a date, Corpse Bride?" he asked in a seductive voice.

"Yes, I have," I said, putting the tickets safely in my purse.

"Your father? Or your first cousin?"

"Alexander," I said confidently.

"That's a shame. I would have escorted you. I could have used it for my community service hours."

Trevor handed the cashier a hundred-dollar bill as Matt, Becky, and I made our exit.

On the way home from school, Becky agreed to stop off at Henry's house.

"Billy Boy left something in the backyard. I'll only be a minute," I said, getting out of her pickup truck.

I raced up the driveway. No lights in Henry's house were lit. I peeked into the garage, empty of his parents' cars. Henry and Billy Boy were at Math Club, so the coast was clear.

I hurried past his gigantic pool and gazebo and ran through the pristinely mowed lawn.

I climbed the treehouse ladder, the rungs creaking with every step of my boots. I reached the treehouse deck and inspected the door.

The amulets were gone.

Shortly after sunset, Alexander arrived at my house to find me pacing on the front walkway.

I kissed him, bursting to tell him my news.

"I went to the treehouse. The amulets—they're gone!" I proclaimed, leading him inside. "Valentine has been back to the treehouse."

"Then we can set a trap. This time, I'll be waiting," Alexander said.

Alexander was giving me a huge squeeze when Billy Boy burst through the front door.

"Look what Henry and I found at the treehouse," my brother declared. In his smarmy little palm he held two shining amulets.

My heart dropped. "Those aren't yours!"

"Well, they certainly aren't yours. Finders keepers."

"Let me see those," I said, reaching for them.

"Here," he said, holding the clasps and letting the amulets swing, as if trying to hypnotize me. "See with your eyes, not with your—"

I tried to grab them, but my brother pulled them away.

"There were four," I said.

"How do you know?"

"Uh . . . amulets come in four; don't you know anything?" I stumbled.

"Henry kept the other two."

"Well, I think they are more my style than yours. Let me have them."

"Forget it. It looks like they're filled with blood," Billy Boy said with delight. "Henry plans to test them."

I paused.

"Then what will you do with them?"

"Use them for our Project Vampire."

That night, Billy Boy and Henry were hunkered in our family room, eagerly doing their vampire project while I was making the finishing touches to my hair.

I heard the doorbell ring.

"I'll get it!" I hollered.

I checked myself out in the hallway mirror. I made sure my teeth were lipstick-free and tightened my black lace sash around my waist.

I opened the door to find my dream guy, looking sexy in a shadowy oversized black shirt, silver-seamed black jeans, and combat boots riddled with straps.

Alexander pulled me to him and gave me a hello kiss.

"Alexander's here! I'll see you later," I called to anyone who was listening, and closed the front door behind me.

"Fortunately Billy Boy's in for the night," I said when I reached Alexander's waiting car. "Who does homework on Friday?"

"There's nothing wrong with being studious," Alexander defended, holding the door open for me.

"It is when the ultrastudious one is my brother," I said, half teasing. "I've always wanted a cool brother. Cryptic, clever, dangerous. Not a nerdy one. But I suppose Billy Boy's always wanted to have an honor student for an older sister, so I guess we're even."

I settled into the Mercedes and Alexander pulled out of the driveway.

"Did Ruby come over for dinner the other night?" I asked, checking my eyeliner in the rearview mirror.

"Yes. The old guy is getting to be quite the ladies' man. It's getting harder for me to borrow Jameson's car. He lent it to me for this evening, but he is taking Ruby out tomorrow night."

"So where are you taking me?" I asked.

"It's a secret. And I have a surprise for you when we get there."

Alexander drove through downtown and toward the outskirts of Dullsville.

"I found this place last night," he said as he turned the car around a tight bend. "I discovered it when I was looking for Valentine. I thought we could grab a few minutes just for us."

Just us. A stolen moment when Alexander and I could finally have a romantic interlude with stars twinkling and the moon shining down on us, and we wouldn't have to worry about Jagger, Luna, Trevor, Valentine, or Billy Boy. I think we'd both been waiting for a chance like this forever.

The car lights illuminated fog as it began to creep over the twisting road, eventually puffing against the car and making it seem like we'd driven through a ghost.

I peered out the passenger-side window, out into the distance. In the darkness, a white billowy haze hung over the desolate fields.

Alexander pulled off onto a dirt road. I could barely see anything in front of us. The car bumped along the unmarked path. We were surrounded by darkness and a fog-covered meadow.

"How can you even see where we are?" I asked.

Alexander seemed confident. He stopped the car and shifted the gear into park.

"I thought we could take a moment to enjoy some-thing new," he said as we got out of the Mercedes.

Alexander grabbed his backpack from the trunk and threw it over his shoulder. He held my hand and gave me a flashlight.

Together we walked through the meadow, pushing the tall grass out of our way.

In the darkness, I could barely make out what appeared to be a hill until Alexander had me shine the flashlight in its direction.

The hill had a huge opening. It was a cave.

"I thought this was just an urban legend!" I exclaimed. I felt as if we were explorers discovering a new land.

"I've heard that as a club initiation kids spend the night here, never to return," I gossiped. "But I never knew it really existed."

I held on to Alexander's belt and followed him into the cave. He could see where he was going in the dark, but he thoughtfully took the flashlight and illuminated the way for me.

We entered the monster-sized mouth of the cave, with its damp, musty scent and distinctive chilly air. The rocky floor was wet, and Alexander steered me clear of any protruding edges. I ran my hand along the side of the cave. Some areas were smooth, some were bumpy and riddled with cavities, while others were covered with moss.

As Alexander led me deeper into the cave, I could hear the faint and soothing sounds of trickling water. When he shined his light above us, an enormous ceiling dripping with stalactites, hanging like gigantic vampire fangs, was revealed.

Alexander led me to a dry spot and passed me the flashlight. I watched as he opened the backpack, pulled out candles, and placed them around us. One by one he lit them, encircling us with candlelight.

"This is the most romantic thing I've ever seen!" I said.

The candles cast shadows from the stalactites and stalagmites against the cave walls, making them seem twice their size. I loved it.

Alexander pulled out a few sandwiches and sodas from his bag. We drank, kissed, and laughed.

As Alexander put the wrappers in his backpack, we heard fluttering sounds above us and spotted a few bats flying overhead.

"They come in and out during the night with food," Alexander said.

"Could Valentine have been one of those bats?"

Alexander didn't respond.

"Tell me more about Valentine," I asked curiously, resting back on my elbows.

"Figures. I bring a beautiful girl to a romantic candlelit cave and she wants to talk about a much younger man."

"You're right," I said in a flirtatious whisper. "Let's talk about us."

"Let's not talk at all," he said in a soft voice.

Then, one by one, Alexander blew out the candles until only one remained.

He paused over the last one, staring at me with a sexy grin, shadows dancing around his handsome face. "I'm making a wish."

"It only comes true on a birthday cake. Besides, you'll be able to see and I won't. It's not fair."

"I'll close my eyes, I promise."

"Not so fast—"

I slid off the black lace sash I was wearing as a belt and loosely tied it around his head, gently covering his eyes. "Now we are equal."

Alexander blew out the last candle.

We were in total darkness. I couldn't see Alexander, the mouth of the cave, or even my own fingers.

Alexander kissed the back of my hand, slowly pecking his way up my arm until he reached my neck.

I paused. "What is the surprise?" I asked. "Are we on sacred ground?"

"Want to find out?" he asked with a smile. "Wait one minute."

A surprise, I thought. *What could it be?*

I felt a warm grasp on my neck.

It was then that I knew. My fantasy was finally coming true. Alexander was going to bite me.

My heart began to pulse against the flesh of his palm. I started to visualize my new life as his hand lay on my most vital of veins.

My dream was to become a vampire, for Alexander to be the one who turned me and be the one to whom I'd be bonded for eternity. But as he held my neck, I suddenly wasn't sure if I was ready to plunge myself into the darkness forever. Thoughts of my parents flooded through me. It was one thing to be an outcast in my own family because I was a Goth. It would be quite another to be an outcast because I was no longer a mortal. I wouldn't be included in family photos, or far worse, I might not be able to see them again in order to keep my new identity a secret. My heart began to race so hard, it almost hurt. It was as if Alexander could feel my soul with his palm. I didn't feel comforted, even by his warm touch.

I'd envisioned an elaborate and gloomy gothic covenant ceremony in Dullsville's cemetery underneath the crystal moonlight, an antique candelabra and a pewter goblet atop a closed coffin, my gorgeous vampire-mate awaiting me by the medieval altar. I'd be holding a bouquet of dead roses and wearing a morbidly black sexy lace dress, which would flow behind me as I walked between the tombstones. We'd join hands and toast to our union, and when I was ready, Alexander would kiss me on the neck.

I hadn't envisioned it this way though, a surprise life-changing moment where I couldn't even see what was happening.

It was as if he knew everything I was thinking—every thought I was feeling was flowing through to his hand. My blood boiled. My head began to spin and I became dizzy.

"Alexander—you are hurting my neck."

"I'm not touching your neck," I heard him say from a distance. "I'm trying to find my backpack."

I gasped. It seemed as if time stood still.

If Alexander wasn't holding my neck, who was?

My dizzy mind was jolted back to reality. "Get off!" I cried. "Let go!"

I flailed my arms and kicked my legs, whacking something or someone. I could hear a stumbling and then a thud.

"Alexander," I called. "We're not alone!"

Who knew who could be lurking in the cavern with us. Maybe as a joke, Trevor had followed us. Or worse, a group of juvies or derelicts were hanging out in the cave. How could a vampire and his mortal girlfriend fend off a gang of sauced-up criminals or delinquent teens defending their turf?

My mind and heart raced. I could barely breathe.

"Alexander—where are you? I can't see!" I continued to flail about but made contact only with the air.

Just then I saw a flash of light. Alexander was before me, his hair messy from removing his blindfold, the flashlight in one hand and my sash in the other. I ran over to my boyfriend and hid behind his back. I grabbed the flashlight, as much to use as a weapon as a source of illumination.

My heart continued to beat as if it were going to jump out of my chest. I shined the light around us. I didn't see anyone. We were alone.

I heard a fluttering sound. Alexander pointed above me. I fixed the light on a single bat hovering over me, his green eyes piercing my soul.

"Alexander—"

Suddenly the bat flew toward the mouth of the cave.

My boyfriend and I quickly chased after the winged creature, back through the cave, carefully running over the slippery rock floor.

By the time we reached the opening, the bat was gone.

On the ground, at the entrance of the cave, something shimmered in the moonlight. Alexander picked up the shining object in his pale hand.

It was an empty amulet.

The following morning, before first bell, Becky and I were hanging out in the main office. I was sitting cross-legged in the secretary's chair, nursing a Styrofoam cup of store-bought java while Becky was eagerly copying valentines for prom.

My once super-silent, shadowy best friend had been selected from the Prom Decorating Committee list to volunteer her time. For some reason, she was volunteering *my* time too.

"We need at least a hundred more," she said, retrieving a stack of pink hearts from the copy tray before they overflowed and handing them to me.

"A hundred?" I whined.

"And then we have to cut them."

"This is the first time I'm actually looking forward to first bell ringing," I said, gazing up at the sluggish office clock.

Every flash of the copier was like lightning striking my already aching head.

"Why are you so tired?" Becky asked. "Did you and Alexander stay out too late on a school night?"

I couldn't reveal to even my best friend the true reason I was exhausted. It wasn't because Alexander and I had had a romantic late evening but rather because I'd tossed and turned all night, thinking about the harrowing events in the cave.

I was conflicted. First of all, had the strange hand on my neck really been Valentine's? I was still uncertain who, or what, had been in the cave with us. And if it had been Jagger's sibling, I could have been moments away from being attacked by a vampire. Secondly, when I thought it was my own vampire boyfriend who was going to bite me, I didn't react the way I'd thought I would. Instead, I panicked. I guess I wasn't as ready as I'd led myself to believe.

Either way, Alexander's surprise and the romantic interlude in a candlelit cave was spoiled. "I'll save it for another time," was all he said when he drove me home.

"I didn't sleep," I finally admitted to Becky. "I'm always keyed up after a date with Alexander."

"Isn't this awesome?" she said with a bright smile. "Not only are we going to prom, but we're helping with the decorations. Who knew?"

How could I get excited about paper hearts when my own real one was throbbing so hard? The most important dance of the year had been miles away from my thoughts. Instead, I was preoccupied with Valentine's whereabouts.

Jennifer Warren, the snarky varsity cheerleader who had snagged my prom dress right in front of my charcoal-stained eyes, strolled through the office door in a red and white pleated skirt and matching shell uniform, her blond ponytail bouncing along after her. She greeted the office workers and marched straight in our direction.

Jennifer was best friends with Heather Ryan, the Prada shoe snob. I figured the two teen fashionistas had conversed, but I hoped it was too early in the morning for another confrontation about designer pumps.

Jennifer ignored me and addressed Becky. "Are you the one who volunteered to make the prom valentines?"

Becky straightened up like a ballerina. Her eyes lit up and her face flushed apple red, as if she had just been greeted by the Queen of England. At any moment, I was ready for my best friend to curtsy.

"My name is Becky," she said, ignoring the copy machine behind her.

Jenny brandished a sparkling smile. "I see you've made a lot of progress already," she remarked, genuinely delighted. "I didn't think you'd start making them until tomorrow."

"Becky is the early worm personified," I complimented.

Jenny posed like a pop star, the flashing copier as her paparazzi. "I always use the best," she said, proud of her new disciple.

Becky beamed as if she'd been chosen for Prom Queen rather than selected to make Xeroxes for a dance.

However, it was clear to me why my best friend was really smiling. Not only was Becky dating Matt Wells, a soccer player, but she was fitting in with cheerleaders and the student body. I was surprised at how easily the once-shy Becky was accepted by the "in" crowd, while I remained solo in the "out" crowd.

"And Raven is helping too," Becky added gleefully.

Jenny looked at me as if I were mud she'd discovered underneath her bright white cheerleading sneakers on a rainy game day. "Uh . . . let me have those," Jenny said, taking the stack from my hands. "I'll start cutting them in study hall."

That was my contribution to the decorating of prom—holding copied valentines for all of ten seconds.

That night, Billy Boy and Henry were locked safely away in my brother's room doing research on the Internet for their Project Vampire. Meanwhile, in my room, Alexander patiently quizzed me on ancient Greece.

I don't know which made it more difficult to study—Alexander's presence or being preoccupied with Valentine's motives and location.

Obviously, Alexander, too, was concerned about Valentine's location and motives, as I frequently caught him peering out the window.

When I suggested we put down my homework and return to the cave, Alexander was firm. "It is best that you and Billy stay inside for a night or two while I figure some things out."

Alexander occasionally gave me stolen kisses before he returned to glancing out the window, and I pretended to be buried in my textbook.

After an arduous day of quizzes, homework hand-ins, and boring lectures, eighth bell rang. I met Becky by our lockers and, after Matt gave her a quick peck before soccer practice, we were off to her house for a prom fashion show.

Becky resided on what many of the snotty Dullsvillians called the "wrong side of the tracks." I, however, thought she had primo real estate. Becky's backyard was twice the size of Trevor's and sported sweet apple trees instead of unused Jacuzzis.

Her farmhouse, built in the 1930s, was the original house her father grew up in. In back of the house, next to the five-acre apple orchard, stood a monstrous silo with vines clinging to it like a giant spiderweb. Adjacent to that sat a red barn filled with tools and a loft suitable for telling ghost stories.

Becky's house was also steeped in character, something

lacking in many of the "right side of the trackers'" houses, including mine. The wooden house was pale yellow with hunter green shutters. It had screen doors and a stellar wraparound porch with an old-fashioned porch swing. Though some of the appliances had been updated, the original yellow flowered wallpaper from her father's youth remained. A round vinyl booth instead of the typical dinette table and chairs was sandwiched in a kitchen alcove. Black-and-white tiles lined the upstairs bathroom walls and floors. Glass doorknobs glistened on all the doors, instead of brass or pewter ones, and hardwood floors ran throughout the first floor.

We walked up the squeaky wooden staircase to her bedroom. One wall was slanted, making it feel as if her movie star posters were going to reach out and kiss you.

Becky pulled out a wedge that kept her closet door shut. Depending on the weather, the door buckled and wouldn't remain closed, which provided hours of fun for us when we were kids, imagining her room was haunted. She took out a garment bag, unzipping it to reveal a vintage floor-length blue strapless gown.

"It's gorgeous!" I exclaimed.

I searched through Becky's jewelry box while she tried on her dress.

My best friend had transformed into a princess right in front of my eyes. "You look beautiful. Matt is going to drop dead when he sees you."

"You think?"

"I know," I corrected.

"Should I wear my hair up in a twist?" she asked, pulling her layered locks off her neck.

"I don't know much about hair," I said. "If it were me, I'd streak it blue to match the dress. But I think the way you have it up looks fabulous."

For the next hour we finalized her jewelry selection (faux pearl earrings and matching necklace) and shades of makeup (coral blush, passion pink lipstick with matching gloss, and indigo blue eye shadow).

Becky and I were starving, so on the drive to my home, we stopped off at Hatsy's Diner, where we stuffed our faces with cheese fries and Vanilla Cokes and talked nonstop about our heartthrobs. Since my best friend and I had acquired boyfriends, we hadn't had the time to be as glued to each other as we had been in the past. Now that we had recharged our batteries, we got in some major girl time and gossiped for hours. She finally dropped me off after sunset.

I opened the front door to find the first floor empty of family members and the phone ringing.

"I'll get it," I hollered.

I dropped my backpack on the kitchen counter and picked up the phone. "Hello?"

"Raven," Alexander said from the other end. My name rolled off his tongue like smooth chocolate dairy soft serve being licked off a spoon. "How was your day?"

"Same as every day—dreadful until sunset," I replied.

The only thing that kept me going through the day was knowing that atop Benson Hill was the most handsome guy I'd ever seen, my very own vampire-mate, sleeping in a coffin in the dusty attic of a creepy old mansion.

"Should I meet you at the Mansion or are you going to pick me up?" I asked eagerly.

There was silence on Alexander's end.

"What's wrong?" I asked.

"I hate to do this to you . . . ," he said, his voice suddenly serious, "but I have to cancel tonight."

"Cancel?" It hit me like a closing coffin lid. "What's wrong?"

"Jameson has the car . . . and I want to check out the cave and cemetery for Valentine."

"I can ask my mom to drop me off instead."

"I want to do it alone," Alexander said in a grave tone.

"Alone?"

Alexander didn't respond. I knew he didn't want to put me in harm's way again, but that didn't mean I had to like it.

Not only would I be missing a nocturnal adventure, I'd be missing precious time with Alexander. It was bad enough I had to be away from Alexander in the sunlight; I couldn't face being away from him in the moonlight, too.

"I'll make it up to you," he said in a bright voice. "I still haven't given you the surprise I was going to give you at the cave."

For the next five minutes I tried whining, protesting, and attempting my tried-and-true manipulation tactics, but nothing worked. Alexander put his foot down, before he put the phone down.

Then I tried arguing with my mother, but she wouldn't

let me borrow the car. I figured if I used Billy Boy's bike, which had thicker tires than mine, I could meet Alexander at the cemetery before he started for the cave.

I knocked on my brother's door.

"Go away!" I heard my annoying brother say.

"I need to ask you for a favor," I said sweetly.

"I'm busy!"

I slowly cracked open the door. My brother's normally bright room was dark, except for a single desk lamp gently illuminating the room. He was sitting at his computer desk typing away on his keyboard with one hand and holding a gravestone etching in the other. To my surprise, there was someone sitting in a chair next to him—and it wasn't Henry.

I froze. Seated next to Billy Boy was a slightly smaller boy with powder white hair.

I gasped.

As if in slow motion, the vampire boy turned to me.

Two glassy green eyes stared through me.

Valentine looked like he'd been dead for more years than he'd been alive. He had a sullen, cadaverous, and almost handsome ghost white complexion, with soft bloodred lips. His long white shaggy hair hung over his face. He exuded an inner strength and, at the same time, a hint of frailty. Though he was only three-fourths my size and seemed like he could blow over with a gentle breeze, something told me he had the power to withstand the force of a storm.

"What are you doing in here?" my brother asked, rising.

"I didn't invite you in."

"I need to speak with you," I said sternly in a low voice.

Valentine's eyes bored through me. Chills ran down my spine like tiny jabbing icicles.

"Get out. I have company," my brother ordered.

Billy Boy charged toward me. He braced the door with his skinny arms and tried to close it. I stopped it with my combat boot.

"What is he doing here?" I whispered.

"He's spending the night."

My heart skidded to a stop. Spending the night? My brother obviously didn't realize who—or what—he'd invited to share his bedroom.

"He can't stay here," I warned softly.

"I don't tell you when Becky can come over. Since when did you become my mother?"

"Where's Henry?" I asked, stalling. "Shouldn't you have invited him, too?"

"He's staying at his grandmother's."

I glanced back at Valentine, whose green eyes glistened at me hypnotically. He licked his lips, and the light of the desk lamp shined on a small fang.

Like a million strobe lights going off in my head, I realized why Valentine must have come to Dullsville. Jagger and Luna weren't seeking revenge on Alexander anymore—they were seeking revenge on me by threatening my family. And they were sending Valentine to do their bloody work.

"Quit nosing around," Billy Boy said.

"But—"

"Get a life!" he yelled as only a little brother could, and slammed the door in my face.

Billy Boy didn't know Valentine was trying to get a life, too—his.

I paced in my bedroom, my combat boots slamming against the black-carpeted floor, while holding my hissing kitten, who was clearly uptight about our new neighbor.

I had to come up with a plan. Alexander was miles away and I wasn't even certain of his location. Unfortunately he never carried a cell phone. I wouldn't be able to inform him that the very person he was searching for was right here underneath my very own roof.

I took a deep breath. I tried to rack my brain for a strategy. I couldn't leave the house with a vengeful vampire in my brother's bedroom. However, my parents would think I had inhaled glue if I ran downstairs and calmly explained to them that Billy Boy had mistakenly invited over a bloodthirsty descendant of Dracula instead of a new-to-town tween in need of a friend.

I'd have to face this problem head-on.

I found my mother in the kitchen placing a plastic tablecloth over our dinette table. "Mom, we need to talk. That friend of Billy Boy's—he can't stay."

"Why not?"

"Word on the street is he's trouble."

"Thank you for your concern, but I'm not worried about an eleven-year-old boy."

"We barely know this kid. He's a stranger."

"What's there to know? He seems delightful and very charming. I think it's good for Billy to widen his circle of friends. He's coming out of his shell."

Billy Boy would be coming out of more than just a shell if Valentine stayed. He could be coming out of a coffin.

"Do you mind setting the table?" she asked as she filled a plastic cup with ice from the door of the fridge.

I grabbed plastic silverware and paper plates from our pantry.

This game wasn't over. I wasn't ready to fold. I had no choice. I had to show my cards.

The ice maker roared thunderously as my mom filled another cup with ice. I put my hand on the granite counter-top and leaned in to my mother. "Valentine thinks he is a vampire."

"What?" she asked, placing the cup on the countertop and beginning to fill another.

"Valentine thinks he's a vampire," I said louder.

"I can't hear you."

I placed my hand over the cup. A few cubes bounced off my knuckles and flew to the floor.

"Valentine has to leave. He thinks he's a vampire," I repeated.

My mom paused. Then she laughed, picked up the fallen cubes, and threw them into the sink.

"Then he should be friends with *you*, not Billy," she remarked playfully.

"I'm serious."

"Serious?" she asked. "Am I talking to the same person I raised, who at five years old wore a black cape around the house because you were imitating Count Dracula? Who at nine insisted on drinking only raspberry Kool-Aid because you thought it resembled blood? And who, just a few days ago, bought a prom dress that resembles a vampire's bridal outfit?"

My mouth dropped open. Touché. My mother's straight flush beat my full house.

"I think it's wonderful that Billy Boy is accepting someone who is different from himself," she continued. "Someone who reminds him of his sister. I'd think you would be flattered."

The doorbell rang.

My mom grabbed a twenty lying on the kitchen counter, and I followed her to the front door. "The pizzas are here!" she called upstairs.

Billy Boy raced down the stairs, Valentine slowly trailing after him like a ghostly shadow.

Valentine stood on the stairs, his black painted fingernails tapping against the wooden banister. He was intently fixated on me, grinning like a gothic Dennis the Menace. I glared back at the four-foot ten-inch vampire as Billy grabbed the pizzas and my mother paid the delivery woman.

Valentine deliberately brushed by me, sending an icy

chill through my body as the two boys flew into the kitchen.

I grabbed a soda from the table and sat down next to my brother.

Billy Boy shot me an odd look. "What are you doing here? Don't you have a hot date?"

"If I did, I wouldn't tell you."

The boys each grabbed a slice of pizza, scarfing it down before it had time to hit their paper plates.

I rose and opened the refrigerator door. "Want some garlic with that?" I asked Valentine, holding up a clove.

It was as if all the blood had drained from Valentine's already pale face. He laid the crust on his plate and sat back in his chair. "Uh . . . no, thank you. I'm deathly allergic to garlic."

"Really? So is Raven's boyfriend," my mother said. "Raven, put that back!"

Reluctantly I returned the clove to the crisper and washed my hands in the kitchen sink.

Valentine glared at me as his morosely ashen complexion turned back to ghostly white.

"Here, take another slice," my mom said, kindly handing Valentine more pizza. He returned to wolfing down his dinner like he hadn't eaten in centuries.

Valentine wiped his tomato-sauce-stained mouth with a napkin and guzzled a soda just like any mortal his age. It was odd to see a boy so young have the potential to be so dangerous. My eyes were glued to him, making sure all he bit into was the pizza.

"Are you visiting or did you move here?" my mom asked.

"Visiting. But I really like this town," he said, looking straight at me.

"Who are you visiting?"

"Uh . . . my aunt, but you wouldn't know her."

"In this town? We know everyone."

"Yes, who is she?" I questioned. "I'd love to meet her." Valentine paused.

"Let us eat," Billy Boy said. "We're hungry."

"You're right, go ahead," my mother said in an apologetic voice.

The boys continued to shovel in their pizza while I observed their every bite. For once in my life, I was the one gawking.

"You are creeping me out," my brother finally said, scooting away from me.

"Raven, let's go in the other room," my mother instructed.

"But—"

She grabbed our plates of half-eaten pizza and we sat in the dining room. All the while I spied on Valentine, keeping my peripheral vision set on the pizza-partying vampire.

I hated that Billy Boy no longer wanted the Madison women hovering around him. He should have listened to me about Valentine. He was beginning to remind me of someone who didn't take orders, someone I knew very well—me.

* * *

Later that evening, while Mom and Dad were downstairs watching TV, I made believe I was folding towels in the hall closet while Valentine brushed his teeth.

The door finally opened and Valentine emerged. He was smiling, his green eyes sparkling, seemingly relaxed in his new environment, until he spotted me in the hallway. Then he glared up at me.

"Did you make sure to floss between your fangs?" I whispered.

"Go ahead, tell your parents," he challenged. "I'll tell them about Alexander," he whispered back, then disappeared into my brother's room.

I stepped into the bathroom. Mom's makeup mirror was facing the wall, and a lavender bath towel was haphazardly placed over the sink mirror.

I could hear my mother whistling as she ascended the stairs.

I quickly retrieved the towel and threw it into the wicker hamper.

"Lights out, boys," my mom ordered, holding a handful of catalogs.

"No, leave the lights on!" I shouted, running into my brother's room. I was hoping an illuminated bedroom would keep Valentine at a safe distance from my brother.

The two boys looked at me strangely.

"The other night, Billy Boy thought he saw a bat," I explained. "I want him to get a good night's rest."

My brother's nerdy white face turned bloodred. I

almost felt sorry I'd embarrassed him in front of his friend.

"Mom, get her out!" he yelled.

My mom shooed me out of the room with her catalog collection and closed the door behind her.

I paced in my room, wondering what Valentine was going to do all night. He obviously wasn't going to sleep. I feared at any moment he might sink his fangs into my brother.

I had no choice. Valentine couldn't sleep here, especially when I knew he wouldn't be sleeping. I didn't have much time; Billy Boy would soon be defenseless. When my brother was a baby, he wailed throughout the night. Now that he was older, he fell asleep as soon as his head hit the pillow.

I raced to my dresser drawer and stuck my container of garlic in the waistband of my skirt.

I crept over to Billy Boy's room. I took a deep breath and cracked his door open.

I wasn't prepared for what I saw. Valentine, his eyes closed as if in a trance, was standing over my sleeping brother, his palm resting on my brother's neck!

"What are you doing?" I said sharply.

Valentine, startled, quickly pulled his hand away.

I gasped. "It was you in the cave," I managed to say.

Valentine remained in place, his fists now clenched.

"I know what you're thinking . . . ," he said in a challenging voice. "I know all about you."

I was confused. "Know what about me? From Jagger and Luna? You can't trust what they say . . ."

He inched forward. "You are afraid."

"Of you?"

He snickered. "Of Alexander."

I folded my arms skeptically. "I love Alexander."

Then Valentine turned deadly serious. "You are afraid of becoming a vampire," he said.

I froze.

"Jagger and Luna didn't have to tell me," he continued. "I learned that from you."

"I don't know what you mean."

Valentine didn't seem to be threatened by my sleeping brother.

"In the cave," he continued. "Alexander wasn't going to bite you. But you thought he was—and you freaked out."

"I don't know what you are talking about."

Then Valentine drew closer, his green eyes locking on to mine in a strange hypnotic stare. "You'd imagined an elaborate and gloomy gothic covenant ceremony in the cemetery, underneath the moonlight, an antique candelabra and a pewter goblet atop a closed coffin."

I stood frozen as the boyish Nosferatu continued to recite the very thoughts and feelings I had had last night at the cave. "You expected to be holding a bouquet of dead roses and wearing a morbidly black sexy lace dress, which would flow behind you as you walked between the tombstones."

How did Valentine know what I had imagined? I could barely breathe as Valentine took another step toward me.

I hadn't told anyone about my dream covenant. Valentine and Billy Boy must have rummaged through my journal—only I didn't even remember writing about my fantasy gothic underworld wedding.

"When you thought Alexander was ready to turn you, your blood ran cold," Valentine charged.

A chill ran from the top of my scalp down through my spine and over the back of my legs.

Valentine had read my thoughts as he stood over me in the cave holding my neck. Now, in Billy Boy's bedroom, he was doing the same thing to my brother. What was he after?

"It is time you leave this house and this town," I said, reaching for my container of garlic.

Like any pesky mortal kid, Valentine enjoyed our quarrel. "You act big with your black nail polish and lipstick, but you could never be one of us. You don't have what it takes," he continued. "And Alexander needs to know you aren't ready."

His words hit me like a lightning bolt. "You can't . . . use my thoughts against me," I warned.

"Or can I?" he asked with a wicked grin.

Billy Boy began to stir.

Valentine quickly retreated into the room's shadows.

I glanced at my brother, who remained sleeping. When I turned back, I noticed Billy Boy's window was open and Valentine was gone.

Blood Reader

V alentine's words haunted me as I futilely attempted to
search through my Olivia Outcast journal for any
covenant dream entries.

"Alexander needs to know you aren't ready," the mischievous vampire had said to me. Valentine was trying to
threaten Billy Boy and at the same time destroy my relationship with Alexander.

I shivered, recalling Valentine's grasping my sleeping
brother's neck. Although I was relieved the tween bloodsucker had escaped from our house, I was still distraught.
I gazed out my window and imagined Valentine flying
directly to the Mansion, squeezing his bat-shaped body
through a breech in an attic window, then becoming a
gothic boy again and confronting an unsuspecting
Alexander with negative ideas about his vampire-wannabe
girlfriend.

If Valentine betrayed my wandering thoughts and

revealed them to my vampire-mate, what would this mean for my future relationship with Alexander? How dare Valentine tell me, much less anyone, that I was frightened of the one thing I'd always dreamed of becoming. On numerous occasions, Alexander made me aware of his disapproval of my joining his dark and dangerous world. My gentle vampire wanted to protect me from the underworld, but gradually, through our time together, he felt comfortable enough to share portions of it with me—the Mansion, the amulets, his coffin. If he knew I had hesitated or, worse, was afraid, he may have no choice but to bond eternally with a true vampire.

Right now, Valentine might be meeting Alexander. I'd sneak out—only I had no way of knowing to where . . . the Mansion, the cemetery, or the cave? I lay in bed, my eyes wide open. I was as restless not knowing where Valentine had flown off to as when the menacing vampire had appeared in Billy Boy's bedroom.

The next morning, I awoke to the sounds of Billy Boy's shrill voice rattling through the heating vents. I lifted up my groggy head from the pillow, grabbed my Malice in Wonderland slippers, and headed downstairs.

My parents were brunching on coffee and cantaloupe while reading the Dullsville Saturday newspaper.

"Valentine is gone," Billy Boy, still in sweats and an oversized T-shirt, ranted to my parents. "He wasn't here when I woke up. He didn't even say good-bye."

"Are you sure?" my mother asked. "Did you check the entire house?"

"I searched everywhere."

My parents looked concerned. "Did you call him at his house?"

"I don't have the number," Billy Boy replied.

They don't have a phone in the bat cave? I wanted to say.

"Maybe we should drive by his house," my dad offered.

"He said he was staying with his aunt, but I don't know where she lives," my brother confessed.

I had to put a stop to this before my parents involved the police, the PTA, and Dullsville's mayor.

"Why is there so much commotion?" I chimed in. "I saw Valentine get picked up last night after everyone went to sleep. I guess he was homesick. I thought you all knew."

"He didn't tell me—," Billy Boy said.

"Duh—he obviously was too embarrassed. He wants to impress you, not look like a fool."

"In elementary school," my mother began, "I had a friend who frequently came over with her sleeping bag, but always left by ten-thirty."

Billy Boy shrugged and said, "Maybe you're right." He grabbed a cup of juice and headed upstairs. I followed him to his room and stood outside the doorway.

"What were you doing on the computer last night?" I asked.

"What's it to you?"

"Don't be annoying. Hey, if it wasn't for me, you'd be searching the crawl space for your friend."

Billy Boy rolled his eyes, then sighed. "Okay. We were looking for tombstones."

"That sounds like something I'd do."

"Well, maybe we are more alike than you think."

I checked out my brother, who was sporting a Chess Club T-shirt. "That'll be the day. Why were you searching for tombstones?"

Billy pulled something out of his desk drawer. "Valentine had these," he said, revealing a weathered piece of paper.

Billy Boy showed me a cryptic gravestone etching— just like the ones Jagger used as grim artwork to decorate his hideouts.

"Valentine said these were his ancestors," Billy Boy continued. "These two are from Romania. We were searching for the last one when you burst in. Now I can't find it."

"Let me see them."

"No, I need to return these to Valentine when I see him again."

"When do you plan on meeting him?"

"None of your business."

"It *is* my business unless you want to find someone else to protect you from bats hanging on your windowsill," I threatened.

Billy Boy appeared aghast, recalling the wiry creature dangling just outside his bedroom.

"Monday at Oakley Park's fountain. After dinner."

"Let me see the etching!"

"No."

"Pretty please, with bat wings on top?"

"We're going to put it with our vampire project."

Billy Boy slammed the door before I could wedge my foot in. Then he bolted the door. Not only was Valentine becoming more brazen, so was my nerdy brother.

I opened my eyes to eternal darkness in Alexander's coffin. I'd been sound asleep for what seemed like centuries next to my vampire-mate. I could hear gentle breathing next to me. I stretched out my arms and hit the lid of the closed coffin. I wasn't entwined in Alexander's arms, but rather pressed against his back.

Unaware of the time, I gently nudged my sleeping vampire. I wanted to know how much longer we'd be entombed.

I heard my boyfriend stir.

"Alexander?"

I could feel his body turn over. His hand gently rested against my neck.

"Reading my thoughts?" I asked. "Hmm . . . I bet you can't guess what I'm thinking," I teased coyly.

Alexander didn't remove his hand. Instead he pressed harder.

My heart rate quickened. I became dizzy. I felt claustrophobic, like the already close coffin walls were closing in on us.

"Alexander—"

His hand only gripped me harder.

Then I realized, it wasn't Alexander's hand holding

my neck. "Valentine," I cried. "Get off!"

I desperately reached for the coffin lid. I pushed and banged, but the lid must have been locked. I scrambled, clawing my nails into the wooden lid.

I called out again, "Alexander!" But there was no answer.

I tried breathing slowly, but that only made me gasp for air. I pounded on the coffin lid. I wedged my boots against the lid and pressed against it with all my might.

"Let me out!" I tried to say, but no words escaped me.

The lid flew open.

I squinted my eyes, trying to adjust to the light.

I wasn't prepared for what I saw—Valentine was standing above me next to the casket, a candelabra glowing behind him.

If Valentine was standing outside the coffin—who had been in the coffin with me?

Slowly, I turned back.

Billy Boy was resting on his arm. He grinned, flashing his newly formed fangs.

"No!" I cried. "Not my brother!"

I woke up with a scream to find myself crashed out on our family-room couch. *House of Dracula* was playing on the TV. The cable box flashed its green neon light. The clock read later than I thought—the moon was on the rise.

As the sun began to set, streaks of purples and pinks hung across the sky, forming a magical sunset. I arrived at the Mansion, ran up the winding driveway and the cracked, uneven Mansion steps, then rapped on the door with the heavy serpent-shaped door knocker.

No one responded. I rapped on the door again.

Finally the door slowly creaked open. Standing to one side, Jameson, in his black butler's uniform, greeted me with a skinny-toothed smile.

"Hello, Miss Raven. I'm afraid Alexander is not ready for company."

"I know, but I have to see him as soon as he's ready. Can I wait inside?"

"Of course. Come in. You may wait in the drawing room," the creepy man said, and pointed to the room where I had awaited Alexander for our first dinner together. The room appeared the same, with an antique European desk, dusty ancient scarlet velvet upholstered chairs, and a baby grand piano in the corner. "Did you know that originally parlor rooms were for the family to view the deceased?" he said as only a creepy man could.

"Interesting," I said as I stepped into the room and imagined what corpses might have been hanging out in here.

"Can I get you something to drink while you wait?" the butler asked me.

"No, thank you. I didn't mean to bust in here early."

"Please, make yourself comfortable. I'd entertain you, but I have to get ready. Miss Ruby is picking me up for dinner tonight."

With that, the creepy man's bulging eyes twinkled and he disappeared from the room.

I opened the small desk. Inside was a box of centuries-old stationery marked STERLINGS and a dried-out Montblanc pen. It would be a dream come true to someday live here with Alexander and Jameson. I surely wouldn't change anything—maybe just add a slightly feminine touch. Vases of dead black roses, portraits of Alexander and me, scented lavender votives scattered throughout the Mansion.

It seemed like forever as I waited for my vampire to arise from his cozy casket. Impatience shot through me. I felt as if I were a groupie waiting backstage for a rock star.

I pulled back the heavy velvet drapes and rubbed my hand against the dusty window. I peered out as the sun slowly set over the horizon. Seconds seemed like a lifetime, minutes like eternity.

"Alexander will see you now," Jameson finally said, now dressed in a gray evening suit.

My combat boots couldn't carry me fast enough up the grand staircase. I raced past the million rooms and up Alexander's creaky attic stairs hoping they wouldn't give out on me.

Alexander greeted me in a black ICP tour T-shirt, oversized black pants with a handcuff belt buckle, and black Converse sneakers.

"I saw Valentine," I blurted out before my boyfriend had the chance to say hello.

Alexander stopped. His thick brown eyebrows tensed.

"He was in my house!" I said, half terrified, half excited.

"Did he hurt you—or your family?"

"No."

Alexander seemed relieved, but then became worried. "How did he get in?"

"Billy Boy invited him for a sleepover. He ate dinner with us—pizza. He's sneakier than Jagger."

"While I was out searching the cemetery and cave for him, he was inside your home?"

I nodded.

"Why didn't you get me?"

"I couldn't. I didn't know where you were—or how to find you. You don't carry a cell phone."

Alexander turned away. I could tell he felt responsible.

"Ever since I arrived here . . . I've brought trouble for you and your family. I thought I was leaving the Maxwells behind when I came to live in the Mansion. Now I realize you would have been better off if I'd stayed in Romania."

"Don't say that!" I said, grasping his shirt and pulling him close. "I would never have met you and fallen in love. We wouldn't be together."

I leaned in to his chest, then looked up and kissed him.

His tense body relaxed and his arms melted around my waist.

"Billy Boy and Henry are meeting Valentine tomorrow night at Oakley Park. But tonight my brother is home studying. So for now we are all safe."

Alexander began to smile. "Then let's celebrate."

My boyfriend took me by the hand and led me downstairs and through the unkempt grass of his backyard to the dilapidated gazebo.

"When I come here at night, I wonder what you are dreaming," he said, lighting a half-melted candle resting on the ledge.

"I'm dreaming about you. Except last night, when I dreamed my brother was a vampire."

Alexander leaned back against the decaying wooden structure and stared out into the moonlight. "The Maxwells are disturbing your days and nights."

I cozied up to Alexander and gazed into his midnight-colored eyes. "You know that I want to be with you, no matter who or what you are. I always want you to know that—no matter what anyone might say to you."

"Who would say differently?"

"You never know in this town, with vampires and nemeses running amuck."

"I know exactly how you feel, because it's the same way I feel."

His words warmed the blood that flowed through my veins.

"In the cave, it was Valentine who touched my neck. I found him doing the same to my brother. At first I thought he was planning to bite us." I paused. "Instead, he was reading our thoughts," I continued.

"How do you know?"

This time I didn't answer.

"Valentine is gifted. He's reading more than your thoughts; he is recording your soul. In the Underworld we call him a 'blood reader,'" Alexander explained.

I took a deep breath. I was ready to confess my hesitation—before Alexander heard it from the menacing vampire—that though I'd always wanted to become a vampire, when I thought I was going to be turned, I became confused. "I think Valentine—"

"Enough of him," Alexander said, brushing my hair off my shoulder. "I can read mortals, too," he continued with a sexy smile. "Though I have my own way."

Alexander pressed his lips against mine. I could feel my heart race more quickly than at the touch of any preteen vampire.

The next evening, Alexander refused to let me search for Valentine. Instead he elected to hang out with the Madison family in our home. Like a gothic guardian he kept a watchful eye, ensuring no bloodsucking visitors would skip through our front door.

Observing Alexander protect my unsuspecting family made him even dreamier in my eyes than he already was.

The following day, I spent study hall in the cafeteria. The lunch ladies were sorting trays and preparing meals for four hundred hungry students. The smell of schoolhouse chili filled our study hall. I was stretched out over a table, resting my head against my backpack when I overheard a soccer snob talking to Jenny Warren at the table next to me.

"Did you hear about Trevor?" he asked her.

"No, tell me."

"There was this freaky kid hanging at Hatsy's Diner last night. He kept staring at Trevor and when Trevor confronted him, the kid tried to choke him."

Two majorly thin brunette soccer snob groupies were sitting at a table behind me. "Well, I heard the coffin boy jumped him and held a knife to Trevor's throat," one said.

"I thought it was a lightsaber," replied the other.

"Quiet down there," Mr. Ferguson chided.

By the time I gathered my belongings, I had overheard the same story five different ways.

I rose and walked over to Mr. Ferguson, who was grading English papers. "I need to be excused," I said.

"Why are you taking your backpack?" he asked skeptically. "Are you planning on not returning to study hall?"

"Listen, if I leave it here, students will fill it with garbage."

"That was you?" Mr. Ferguson asked, surprised. "I heard about that the other day in the teachers' lounge."

I rolled my eyes.

"You'll need a hall pass," he said, opening his briefcase.

"That's okay, I already have one," I said, pulling a blank one out of my back pocket.

I hurried down the hall, passing Mr. Wernick, our intimidating security guard, who was sitting on a chair reading *Sports Illustrated*. It was rumored Mr. Wernick used to be a prison guard.

"Raven—," he said, rising.

"I'm going to the ladies' room."

"I'll need to see your hall pass." He slowly rose from his chair as if his legs were not used to carrying his weight.

I unfolded the pass and presented it to him.

"It doesn't have a date on it," he said, glaring down on me.

I was ready for him to read me my rights.

"Really?" I asked, faking shock. "Mr. Ferguson must have forgotten."

Mr. Wernick grabbed a pen from his shirt pocket and signed the pass. "Good for today only."

I took my pass back, annoyed that he had ruined my golden ticket.

I continued down the hallway and turned the corner. I peered into Mr. Hayden's algebra class and noticed Trevor sitting in the fifth row, flirting with a cheerleader.

I hung out in the restroom for what seemed like an eternity and returned to Trevor's class just as the bell rang.

Mr. Hayden's classroom door opened and students burst into the hall.

Trevor, still fixated on the pom-pom girl, whizzed right past me.

"Trevor," I called to my nemesis. But he didn't hear me.

I caught up to him and pulled his backpack strap until it fell off of the soccer snob.

"Hey, jerk!" Trevor spun around and stopped in his tracks. "Oh, it's you."

"As much as I hate to admit it, I need to speak with you."

"Take a number," Trevor said, and walked on.

"What did you do to Valentine?" I asked, catching up to him.

"Who's Valentine?"

"You know who—the Goth kid at Hatsy's."

"Oh, that punk?"

"People are saying he tried to choke you. But I know that's not what happened. Is it?"

"How do you know what he did or didn't do? You weren't even there."

"I just do. Now tell me."

Trevor paused. "It'll cost you." He gazed down at me, his blond eyelashes accentuating his sexy green eyes.

My stomach turned. "Forget it."

"Forgotten." Trevor adjusted his backpack and joined the crowd of walking students.

"No, wait," I said, catching up to him. "Fine. I'll carry your backpack to class," I offered.

Trevor didn't hand over his North Face pack. Instead he turned to me. "Prom. That's what it will cost."

I almost gagged. "I'm not going with you. I'm going with Alexander."

"One slow dance," he said with a grin.

The thought of slow dancing with Trevor in front of all of Dullsville High made me feel like a contestant on *Fear Factor*. However, I needed the info. I stuck my hands in my pockets. "Fine. I'll do it. Now tell me."

Trevor seemed pleased. He leaned against a locker and began to tell me his story. "I was sitting in Hatsy's Diner with my team when this freaky ghost boy walks in. We looked at him as if he'd just crawled out of a grave. The kid didn't make eye contact with anyone as he walked through the diner. When he reached my booth, he suddenly stopped and stared straight at me—like he knew who I was. I'd never seen him before, but then I realized he looked familiar—just like Luna's brother Jagger, only smaller."

"Did he say anything?"

"No, he went to the counter and ordered fries. The kid was a major freak, so I had to check him out."

"What did he say?"

"Nothing, he was busy counting his change. He only had sixty-five cents."

"So . . ."

"He looked emaciated enough as it was, like he barely had enough blood running through his veins. I took out a five and ordered him a Hatsy's meal."

I almost melted. I had no idea Trevor had a nice side. "I'm impressed," I said truthfully. "Then what happened?"

"I said, 'Are you Jagger's brother?' Then he gave me a death stare and asked, 'Are you Trevor?'"

I felt chills run down my spine.

"So I asked him how he knew me, but he didn't answer. Then I asked, 'How's Luna?'"

A twinge of jealousy ran through me. "You still like her?" I asked.

Trevor didn't respond and continued on. "Instead of

answering me, the kid looked at me like he'd just seen a ghost."

"Go on . . ."

"He seemed confused, like he didn't know. Then, all of a sudden, he reached out and he put his hand on my neck."

I was surprised by Valentine's actions. Instead of hiding like he had at the tree house, Valentine was becoming increasingly daring—this time with Trevor.

"Did you hurt him?"

"No, I called him a freak and pushed him away. He grabbed his Hatsy's meal, jumped on his graveyard-themed skateboard, and sped out of the diner. Now let's talk about prom."

"I need to know . . . when he grabbed your neck—what were you thinking about?"

Trevor paused and smiled a sexy grin. "I was thinking that I should have been at the Graveyard Gala with you instead of his sister."

"Really?" I asked, half flattered, half horrified.

"Are you insane? No one puts their hand on me, unless they're a girl."

The bell rang and Trevor stepped into his classroom. "I get to pick the dance," he said, gloating.

I held up my hand, revealing my fingers had been crossed the whole time I'd made the promise.

Instead of being angry, Trevor cracked a smile. He loved our game. And I knew this time he'd come back playing even stronger.

* * *

"Anyone home?" I called out when I arrived home from school.

The house was silent.

"Billy Boy?" I yelled as I roamed through the kitchen and family room. Both areas were empty. I opened the basement door. The light was switched off, but I hollered down anyway. "Billy—are you here?"

I ran up to Billy Boy's room and knocked on his door. He didn't respond. "Nerd Boy—are you in there?"

When I failed to hear a response from calling him his least favorite name, I figured the nerd lab was clear.

Fortunately, my brother didn't have Henry's Mr. Gadget security system and was unable to lock his door from the outside. I gently turned the knob and opened the door.

I began my search for Valentine's gravestone etchings, hoping they would provide a clue to his motives in Dullsville. I quietly scoured my brother's dresser drawers, but all I found were tons of white socks and folded T-shirts. I checked under his bed and pulled out a baseball bat, a chessboard, and an unopened model spaceship, but no gravestone etchings.

I glanced at Billy Boy's *Star Wars* alarm clock. I didn't have much longer until he would arrive home. I rummaged through his desk drawers, filled with pens, computer games, and software.

I turned on his computer. I tried to access his history page to find out what he and Valentine had searched for, but I couldn't log on. I didn't know Billy Boy's password.

If I were Billy Boy, what would my password be?

I typed in "E=MC2" and pressed the RETURN key.

Nothing.

I typed "Maytheforcebewithyou" and clicked on "Enter."

Denied.

Knowing my brother, he probably switched his password every week. Frustrated, I typed in "Billy Boy" and hit RETURN.

Suddenly the computer signed on. Out of all the passwords—I never dreamed my brother would use the nickname I called him. For a moment, I felt flattered.

Then I heard the front door open and my brother start up the staircase. I glanced at Billy Boy's half-open bedroom door. If I bolted now, he might see me race out of the room. If Billy Boy found out I'd been searching his room, I'd be grounded until prom was over. I switched off his computer, but it seemed like forever until it logged off.

"Come on," I anxiously mumbled.

I could hear him coming up the stairs and down the hallway.

Finally the screen went blank.

I flew over to his closet, quietly slid open the door enough for me to squeeze through, and shut it behind me. Once I was safely inside, I cracked it open slightly.

I saw my brother enter his room.

I sandwiched myself between the wall and his coats. His jackets smelled like dirty air from outside, which was odd because Billy Boy spent most of his time inside his room like a hermit or at Henry's indoor laboratory.

I could hear Billy Boy turn on his computer.

Underneath a pair of shoes in front of me, I saw a box marked PROJECT VAMPIRE.

I could hear the pinging sounds of Billy Boy instant messaging.

I quietly opened the plastic case. VAMPIRE'S NOURISHMENT was marked on a Ziploc bag. Inside were the four amulets. Another see-through bag was marked VAMPIRE'S HOME. Inside were two folded gravestone etchings of people's names I didn't recognize. The last bag was marked VAMPIRE. I opened it to find the back side of a three-by-five photo. I turned it over—it was a picture of me.

When I heard my brother leave his bedroom, I poked my head out the sliding door. *Billy Boy must be heading downstairs for a snack,* I thought. I had just a moment to make my escape. I climbed out of the closet and slid the door shut behind me.

I raced through his room and out the door.

Wham! I plowed into my brother head-on.

"What are you doing in my room?" he asked, stunned from our collision.

"What are you doing in the hallway?" I asked, rubbing my bruised arm.

"You were snooping around! What were you looking for?"

"I was doing a project for school and I needed your school picture. It's called Project Nerd."

I disappeared into my room and left my confused brother standing in the hallway.

"Valentine is making his presence known," I told Alexander, who was waiting for me by the Mansion's gate shortly after sunset.

"What do you mean?" he asked, his dark eyes concerned.

"He was at Hatsy's last night."

"You saw him?"

"No, it was all over school. Something strange happened. I guess Trevor still pines for Luna, because he asked Valentine how she was doing."

"What's weird about that?"

Men, I wanted to say. Even after Luna double-crossed Trevor at the Graveyard Gala, her ghost white fairy image was still emblazoned in my nemesis's heart.

"It's weird," I continued, "because Valentine appeared confused. Like Valentine didn't know, himself."

"That *is* strange."

"It gets more bizarre. Valentine grabbed Trevor's neck like he grabbed mine in the cave."

"In the diner? That's really weird."

"I know . . ."

"Valentine is thirsting for something," Alexander said, "and if he's becoming this brazen, who knows what he'll do next."

"I'm not sure what he's trying to find out, but one thing is certain—he's searching for it in Henry's tree house, and through me, Billy Boy, and now Trevor."

* * *

By the time Alexander and I arrived at the Oakley Park fountain, where Billy Boy had told me he'd be meeting Henry and Valentine, the boys were no longer there.

"We don't even have time to make a wish," I said, referring to the lit fountain, where a couple was throwing in a few pennies.

"Where could they be? They couldn't have gone too far."

Alexander led me by the hand and we hurried over to find the swings empty of any mortals, much less middle schoolers.

"There's a stage down there," I said, pointing to an outdoor domed amphitheater. "That's where Luna was waiting for me. They might be hanging out there."

Alexander and I hurried down the grassy hill and hopped over the few small bushes lining the sides of the amphitheater, then darted through the aisles of seats. The darkened stage, barely illuminated by the streetlight, was quiet and appeared empty as we headed around the orchestra pit. Alexander climbed onstage, then offered his hand and pulled me up.

We each searched a wing of the stage. All I found were cluttered chairs and music stands.

By the look on Alexander's face when he met me center stage, he hadn't found anything more than orchestra props on his side.

"We can try the rec center," I suggested.

Alexander nodded. "Point the way."

This time I took my boyfriend's hand and anxiously

hurried back through the theater aisles and up a small hill.

We jogged around the fenced-in tennis courts and adjacent hoopless basketball courts, which had been worn down by years of players' squeaking sneakers. Oakley Park's rec center had seen better days. When Becky and I were younger, we spent many summer breaks hanging by the pool, Becky nursing her tan while I sequestered myself underneath a Hello Batty visor and an oversized umbrella. Now that many Dullsvillians belonged to Dullsville's new country club or the Y, the rec center had deteriorated.

The grungy dirt brown metal doors were locked and the handles were secured with padlocked chains. I leaned my head against the dusty windows. The few offices had their shades pulled closed. I peered into the game room. Several pool tables were still in good shape, while the Ping-Pong table was missing a net.

We heard voices.

"What's that?" I asked, pulling on Alexander's sleeve.

He put his index finger in front of his lips.

The voices seemed to be coming from the pool area.

Alexander crept past the pool gate and empty kiddie pool, now littered with leaves and debris, while I tiptoed close behind him. Who knew who we'd find hanging out at a park after hours.

The crispiest French fries and the best hamburgers in town came right from this snack bar—where now shreds of red and white paint clung for dear life to the rusty metal roof, begging for a paint job when the pool reopened for summer break.

Then I noticed a coffin-shaped skateboard, emblazoned with a white skull and crossbones, and Henry's and Billy Boy's bikes lying near what a vampire might view as a huge vacant grave—Oakley Park's empty swimming pool.

I raced over to the edge of the shallow end and peered into the drained pool with its chipping ocean blue paint.

In the deep end, Henry, Billy Boy, and Valentine were sitting in a circle facing one another, a lit antique candelabra next to them, casting light on their faces.

The boys didn't even notice that Alexander and I were standing only a few yards behind where the diving board used to be. As if in a trance, the nerd-mates seemed fixated on Valentine.

It was then I noticed each boy had pricked his finger with a pin, a bottle of alcohol perched on the pool's edge.

"I really don't think we should do this," my brother said nervously.

"C'mon, it'll be okay," Valentine persuaded.

"Billy's right," Henry added.

"Fine," Valentine said. "But think of this. Neither one of you has brothers, and mine has deserted me. This way we'll all be brothers—blood brothers."

Billy Boy and Henry looked at each other. They seemed to be mesmerized by that idea.

"Blood brothers," Billy repeated.

"For now," Henry said.

"Forever," Billy Boy said.

"For eternity."

"Over my dead body!" I climbed down the shaky silver pool ladder and dropped to the blue cement pool floor.

Alexander took off around the pool deck.

As I raced toward them, I could see the innocent mortals' bloodstained fingers within inches of touching a vampire's. I didn't know the repercussions of their actions, but I assumed they wouldn't be good. I jumped in between them.

"No!" Valentine screamed. "No!"

Valentine caught Alexander's stern glare and started to run up the ascending pool floor to the shallow end, but Alexander grabbed him by the shirtsleeve, stopping the fleeing vampire.

"What's going on?" Billy Boy asked, as if coming out of a daze.

"What are you doing here?" Henry asked me.

"I should be asking you that!" I yelled in a voice that reminded me of my mother's. "Both of you go wash your hands," I ordered. "Make sure you clean them with alcohol, too."

Valentine breathed heavily. "I was so close," he said, wiping his white bangs away from his fierce green eyes.

"What are you trying to do to my brother?" I argued. "What do you mean Jagger deserted you?"

Valentine balled his fists. "Where are Jagger and Luna?" he demanded.

"They're in Romania," I said.

"You are wrong," he said.

"What do you mean?" I asked, confused.

"They haven't returned. And I know you had something to do with it," he said directly to me.

"Raven had nothing to do with it," Alexander said in my defense. "Any grudge your family has is with me."

"Do you know who you're protecting?" Valentine argued. "I knew from the moment I laid my hand on her in the cave—Raven is not ready to turn her mortal life over to you."

Alexander turned to me. His dreamy chocolate eyes turned sad and lonely.

"I never said that," I disputed.

"But you thought it," Valentine said with a cunning grin.

I knew Valentine's piercing comments were like a stake through my boyfriend's heart. Alexander stepped away from me as if registering a moment of utter isolation.

My eyes began to well. "Alexander—"

As Alexander looked at me, Valentine, who was standing on the shallower end, reached for Alexander's neck. I could see his pale fingers clench tightly around my boyfriend's throat.

"Alexander!" I screamed, running toward him.

Valentine closed his eyes as if channeling Alexander's soul into his pale palm.

Alexander's midnight eyes turned red. He spun around and knocked Valentine's hand away. The force sent Valentine stumbling back until he wiped out on the pool floor.

"What are you guys doing to Valentine?" Billy Boy asked from behind me, his voice distressed.

Alexander and I turned to see Billy Boy and Henry standing several feet above us at the pool's edge, shocked.

"Valentine was trying to hurt us," I said.

We turned back to Valentine, who was climbing up the pool ladder. He hopped on his coffin-shaped skateboard and disappeared into the darkness.

13

Alexander and I didn't even have time to discuss the event at the pool. We immediately whisked the nerd-mates into the car and chaperoned them safely home. Once again Valentine had threatened my brother's safety and fled into the night. I wasn't sure when he'd reappear with another plan of revenge.

When Billy Boy and I returned home, I was forced to spill my guts to my parents about my brother's injurious actions. Valentine, like his older brother, Jagger, had a charm that was magnetic, if not hypnotic. The nerd-mates had fallen under the tween vampire's bewitching spell. The only way I could impede their adoration was by involving Sarah and Paul Madison.

"You did *what?*" my mother hollered at Billy Boy when I told her about the blood brothers ceremony. "Do you know how dangerous it is to stick a needle in your finger?"

"We used alcohol," Billy Boy protested.

"But you deliberately tried to mix your blood with your friends' blood," my mother argued. "I thought you were smarter than that."

"I remember back in my day, it was common for boys to become blood brothers," my dad confessed. "Like a rite of passage. However, times have changed, Billy. Now, what seemed like a harmless ritual can be very unhealthy, if not fatal."

"We didn't even touch each other," Billy Boy whined. "Raven jumped in between us."

My mother appeared surprised, then relieved.

"Raven has pierced every inch of her earlobe and she never gets in trouble," my brother argued.

"I take offense to that. I'm in trouble all the time!" I defended myself proudly.

"I don't understand why I'm getting all the heat," Billy Boy said. "Alexander pushed Valentine."

"He did what?" my dad asked.

"Valentine tried to choke Alexander," I explained. "Alexander pushed his hand away, that's all."

"Maybe it's best you and Valentine take a break from each other for a few days," my dad warned.

"You can't do that! He's my best friend!" Billy Boy was enraged. He mumbled something unintelligible and stormed upstairs.

I felt this tense situation was going to get worse before it would ever get better.

* * *

Billy Boy's grounding meant that for the next week he would be safe from Valentine.

However, the next day I stewed in class. Valentine was pursuing more than my brother's thoughts in Dullsville's rec center pool. In addition, Valentine confronted Alexander head-on, not only declaring I was inadequate for my vampire boyfriend, but also trying to read his soul. With every sunset, Valentine was becoming more confrontational, as if he were a grizzly bear hunting for food in a family's backyard.

I couldn't shake the image of Valentine's hand on my boyfriend's neck. I wondered what Alexander's thoughts were. Was he imagining breaking up with me, now that he thought I was a coward? I wondered if he'd regretted his decision not to be with Luna.

Instead of longing for the sunset, I was dreading it. I wasn't sure how I'd ever be able to face my vampire-mate.

At lunch, once again I was desperate to tell Becky everything.

"Why are you so long in the face?" she asked. "Prom is only a few days away."

I wanted to tell her my dilemma. Explain how Alexander had left Luna at their covenant ceremony because he didn't want to take her into the Underworld unloved. Reveal then that Jagger, who followed Alexander to America to seek revenge, met me in Hipsterville and followed me back to my hometown. And now Alexander and I were faced with Jagger and Luna's younger brother, Valentine, who was seeking revenge on behalf of the Maxwell clan. All the while, I was struggling with a big decision: whether to someday face my own mortality—or immortality—by bonding with my vampire-mate for eternity.

I was dying to spell out for my best friend how easy she had it, dating a mortal. Nothing more to decide at the end of the day than what music to download or what television show to watch.

"If I told you something," I began, "and I made you promise not to tell anyone . . . not even your family or Matt, could you do it?"

Instead of Becky eagerly nodding her head, she bit her red chipped fingernail and thought. And thought. And thought.

"This isn't multiple choice. It's a simple yes or no!" I snapped.

"Well, it's more complicated than that."

"How complicated can it be? You can either keep a secret or you can't."

"I'm just not sure."

"I'm your best friend. You should keep a secret just because I asked you."

"I know . . . you're right, but—"

"I've told you a million things before and it was never an issue."

"That was before," she admitted.

"Before what?"

"Before Matt came into my life. I don't think it's healthy to keep secrets from him."

"This secret has nothing to do with him."

"What if it slips out?"

"It can't slip out. It's the most secretest of all secrets. Aren't you even curious?"

"I'd feel funny if I hid something from him."

I was slightly jealous of her sudden allegiance to Matt when it meant leaving me, her best friend, in the dark.

"You think he tells you everything?" I snipped. "From the time he rises to the time he sleeps? Every thought he has? Every song he listens to?"

"That is his choice. Besides, I believe he tells me everything," she said confidently, just as Matt joined us.

"I'm not supposed to tell you this," Matt began, "but a few of the guys on the soccer team have booked a limo for prom."

Becky smiled and gave me a knowing glance.

She was right. I'd have to carry my secret to the grave.

That evening, when I arrived at the Mansion's gate, my usually awaiting vampire was a no-show. I hiked up the long driveway in my Morbid Threads black-and-white-striped tank, black flowered embroidered skirt, black knee-high fishnets, and Black Kitty Mary Janes.

I rapped on the door with the serpent knocker. The Mansion door stood still, as if it were peering down at me, barring me from returning to see my vampire-mate.

I knew it—Alexander was having second thoughts about me.

I walked around the side entrance. The Mercedes was

parked at the detached garage. I knocked again, but no one answered.

I returned to the front door and pounded my fists on the wooden entrance.

I could hear the bolts unlock, and slowly the Mansion door creaked open. Jameson popped his head out.

"Miss Raven, I'm surprised to see you."

"Alexander and I were supposed to meet by the gate."

"I thought you knew, Miss Raven. Alexander's gone."

Gone? My heart felt like it fell out of my chest and dropped between the weed-filled cracks in the Mansion's uneven front steps.

"He moved back to Romania?" I asked, my voice cracking.

"No, he went out for the evening. I thought he was meeting you."

"So did I."

Jameson seemed worried. "Alexander was behaving oddly this evening."

"There's someone he visits when he feels troubled. I think I might know where he has gone," I said.

"Can I drive you somewhere?"

"That would be wonderful!"

Jameson drove the Mercedes as slowly as if he were pushing the car with his feet. I figured by the time we reached Alexander, I'd be as old as the creepy man himself.

Jameson finally parked in front of Dullsville's cemetery.

"I'll just be a minute."

I ran between the tombstones and straight to Alexander's grandmother's monument.

There, crouched by the memorial, was my boyfriend, placing a handful of wildflowers by the grave marker.

"Alexander—"

He glanced up at me, surprised.

"We were supposed to meet at the Mansion," I said.

"I lost track of time. I just came here for a minute to get some wisdom. My grandmother was a wonderful woman. She was different from our family but always longed to be one of us. You remind me of her."

"You don't want us to be together—now that you've heard what Valentine said."

"Now I understand why, when we were at the gazebo, you said you liked me for who I was. You were worried Valentine would say something."

I nodded. "It was just a moment in the cave. If I had known ahead of time, everything would be different."

"Would it?"

"Don't you trust me?"

"I don't trust myself. I've let you into my world far too quickly."

"Please, don't say that."

"I never meant to frighten you."

"Me, frightened?"

"I don't want you to become like me. I've never asked you to join my world. I don't want you to be afraid that I will put you in that position."

I pulled him close. "Please, don't say such things. If

more humans were like you, the world would be a much better place."

"Maybe we are deceiving each other—you thinking you can be a vampire, and me thinking I can be with a mortal."

"Please, this is exactly what Valentine wants. He's trying to take revenge on us by destroying our relationship. We were fine before he came."

Alexander's sullen eyes started to sparkle.

"You are right. I am playing right into his blood-reading hands." Alexander took my hand in his. "I would be nothing, in your world or mine, without you."

Alexander kissed me as Jameson flickered the lights on his car.

14

Morbid Manicure

I have a treat for you girls," my mom said as Becky and I climbed into her SUV the afternoon of prom. "I scheduled two appointments for manicures for your big night tonight."

"Yay!" we both cried out in unison.

"Thank you so much, Mrs. Madison," Becky gushed.

Mindi's, an ultra-swank conservative salon, with its signature bright black-and-white-striped awning, was located in Dullsville's main square, between Fancy Schmancy Gifts and Linda's Lingerie.

"Maybe we can go there, too," I whispered to a blushing Becky when we got out of the SUV, referring to the sexy intimate clothing store.

Becky and I followed my mother into Mindi's chichi salon. The stylists were clad in crisp white tops and black rayon pants.

The chairs were filled with Dullsville High promgoers

getting makeovers, haircuts, and pedicures. All heads—being cut, blow-dried, and colored—turned toward me as if I (clad in tight black zippered shorts, black tights, Frankenstein boots, and a Gothique T-shirt) wasn't worthy of entering the salon.

"Pick out your polish," my mother instructed, pointing Becky and me to a Lucite shelf hanging on the wall next to the hair section. A ton of products lined the white wooden shelves—snazzy accessories in a rainbow of colors and fabrics, combs (skinny and wide-toothed), and brushes (round, flat, and lamb's-bristled). Dozens of shampoos and conditioners for every type of hair—frizzy, curly, straight, dry, oily, thick, and thin—were also displayed. I was amazed at what a bottle filled with soap and a few vitamins and minerals claimed to do. For the prices Mindi's was asking, I'd think they were filled with champagne.

Becky and I perused the nail polish selection while my mother checked us in. The shelves were filled with a spectrum of colors from pink to purple, red to clear. Becky quickly chose a bottle of Pink Persuasion.

I scanned the polishes. Nothing resembled black, not even a deep purple or brown among them.

My mother joined us, buzzing like it was my wedding day. She was exhilarated, caught up in the prom spirit as if she were going herself. Since I had been an outcast for so long, she herself had never been included in the high school's events.

"So what have you decided on, girls?" she asked.

"Becky picked a beautiful pink," I said.

My best friend proudly showed my mother her selection of a pretty pastel nail color.

"Lovely choice, Becky. Raven, what have you picked?"

"Well . . ."

"We're ready for you," a pixie-like girl with spiky short red hair said, her white shirt stretched tightly around her pregnant belly. "I'm Cami."

"I'll pick you up in half an hour," my mom said. "Remember, when the girls have finished, don't touch anything! You don't want to smear your manicure."

Cami led Becky and me past a dozen hairstylists' chairs to the nail room—or what I'd call a vampire's nightmare. The walls were made of mirrors, and bright fluorescent lights filled the ten-by-ten-foot room. Alexander wouldn't last two seconds in here.

A half-dozen white manicure tables—each with a black desk lamp, white hand towels, and pastel polishes—faced the mirrored walls. A few pedicure bowls were sitting on the floor, all occupied by the feet of adolescent fashionistas.

Jenny Warren and her Prada shoe-snob friend, Heather Ryan, sat underneath foils with one foot in a spa bath and the other resting on a pedicurist's lap, their flawless model's toes being primped for their walk down Prom Princess Road.

Cami showed Becky to her seat, then directed me to the vacant chair next to hers. As I settled in, a middle-aged veteran manicurist nodded to me as she stood over her client, whose hands were drying underneath a heating lamp.

Becky and I watched as Cami started removing Becky's nail polish.

"You must be Raven," my manicurist said, placing a plastic finger bowl filled with sudsy water on her table. "I'm Jean."

"Nice to meet you," I responded with a smile.

I glanced over at Becky, who was engaged in conversation with Cami as if they'd been friends for years. Cami looked like she'd just graduated from beauty school.

My manicurist, however, with her crazy colored bifocals, resembled my grandmother. Her own thick nails weren't painted and looked weathered. Who could blame her? By the end of the day, she was probably too exhausted to decorate her own nails.

"What color have you picked?" she asked, looking at me above her bifocals.

"Well . . . I haven't decided yet."

Jean began removing my black polish with a cotton ball. It took her a few minutes to get it out of the nooks, the dark color imbedded in my nails.

"Your mother said your dress was a dark red."

"Yes," I said, our conversation stilted.

Jean opened her drawer and pulled out a bottle of red nail polish. "How about this?"

"I prefer something darker."

Jean placed my hands in the finger bowl filled with warm, bubbly water.

"This color is very popular." She held out a bottle of metallic pink.

"I was thinking of black."

"How about something more feminine," she said, ignoring my request.

I could feel Becky slink down in her chair next to me. Becky and Cami continued to talk but kept eyeballing Jean and me.

Jean rose and went to the front desk. In a moment, she returned with a few bottles of reds and pinks.

"I thought you'd want to look like Cinderella, not Frankenstein," she quipped, placing the colors on her manicure table and sitting down.

"I'd really like black."

"But we don't carry black," she insisted.

"No problem. I brought a bottle with me." I reached for my purse, accidentally dripping water on her desk as I lifted my hand out of the bowl.

Jenny and Heather giggled at me.

"Hold on," Jean grumbled. "Allow me."

Jean mopped up my spills with a hand towel and threw it into a small white wicker laundry basket underneath her desk. She picked up my *Corpse Bride* purse, examined it as if it might bite her, then pulled out a half-filled bottle of Morbid Mayhem.

Jean placed my polish on her desk as if she were holding a bottle of poison. She squeezed eucalyptus-scented lotion on my hand and vigorously massaged it into my skin. She filed, smoothed, and pushed back my cuticles and reluctantly began to paint my nails a morbid black.

"So who are you going to prom with?" she asked.

"My boyfriend."

"Would I know him—or his family?"

"He doesn't go to our school."

"Is he from out of town?"

"No, he's homeschooled."

"That's interesting . . . What's his name?"

This was more like an inquisition than a manicure.

"Alexander Sterling."

"You mean the Sterlings on Benson Hill?" she asked, surprised.

"Yes."

"I've heard about them. They moved into the Mansion a while ago."

"That's right."

"His parents are never around. I was hoping his mother might come into the salon."

"They travel a lot."

"I see. And what is your boyfriend like?"

"He's a lot like me."

"Wears black nail polish?" she teased.

"Sometimes," I said with a smile.

I was beginning to take a liking to ol' Jean, and I think she was warming a bit to me. Not only was she flip and sarcastic like me, but I had something she wanted—firsthand knowledge of new townsfolk I'm sure had been gossiped about in her salon since the day the Munster-like family inhabited the Mansion.

Becky rose and sat with her hands underneath the dryers, leaving me alone in the corner with Jean as she applied a clear top coat to my nails.

"I had a client come in yesterday to get a French manicure," she whispered. "She said she met your boyfriend at a restaurant. She was spreading all sorts of gossip."

"You mean Mrs. Mitchell?"

"I don't like to spread things around," she said seriously.

I bit my black lip to keep myself from laughing.

"After meeting you," she continued, "I can't believe the talk of the town. You are such a dear, and I imagine your boyfriend has to be a gentleman."

I smiled at Jean. "She calls us vampires behind our backs just because we wear dark clothes and nail polish."

"I see . . ."

"She really needs to get a job, that woman."

"Well, I have to be honest, I'd rather see you in red polish, but I think this black is quite striking. I'd order some for the salon," she whispered again, "but I'm afraid you'd be the only one to wear it."

"Keep it," I said as I sat next to Becky and placed my hands underneath the dryer. "Next time Mrs. Mitchell comes in for a French manicure, make it a Romanian one, like mine."

15

Dance with a Vampire

Dullsville High School's prom night—one evening I was lucky I wasn't a vampire. If I had to wait until sunset just to rise from sleep, I'd never have time to shower, fix my hair, change from combat boots to witchy boots, decide between onyx and spiderweb earrings, rework my hair, and reapply my eyeliner. Most important, I would be nothing without a mirror.

I looked like a medieval dark angel. All that was missing was my vampire teeth.

Glancing out the window, I saw Alexander pull Jameson's Mercedes into our driveway. As I reapplied my lipstick and made the final touches to my makeup, I could hear the doorbell ring and mumbled greetings.

"Alexander's here," my mother called up to me.

"I'm coming," I answered.

With one hand I gathered the bottom of my dress, and

with the other I carried my open parasol. I descended the staircase like the bride of Dracula.

Alexander and my parents were seated in the living room.

When Alexander saw me, his eyes lit up and he immediately rose. My heart dropped. He appeared more gorgeous than I'd imagined. Alexander looked like a sexy vampire idol in a silky chic dark suit with a red handkerchief poking out of his breast pocket. His hair hung in his face as his midnight eyes sparkled. He flashed me a sweet smile.

Alexander held his hand over his heart. "You are so beautiful. I believe you've taken my breath away."

He politely kissed me on my cheek. His soft velvet lips sent chills racing through me.

Alexander handed me a black rectangular box.

I opened the box. A red rose with white baby's breath was attached to an elastic lace band with red rhinestones.

"It's beautiful."

"It matches her dress to a tee. How did you know?" my mother asked.

"I want to put it on," I said excitedly.

My mother helped take the corsage out of the box and handed it to Alexander.

"I thought this was safer than sticking you with a pin like I did when we attended the Snow Ball," he said as he slid the corsage over my wrist.

"Billy," my father called. "Come down and see your sister."

"We have to take pictures," my mother gushed.

"No!" I said.

My parents looked at me oddly.

"It's bad luck."

"What are you talking about? Generations of people have taken pictures of their proms and have them in photo albums for years. It's a tradition," my mother corrected.

Alexander's eyes turned sorrowful. I could tell he felt he was denying me memories to cherish for a lifetime.

He grabbed my hand. "Mrs. Madison, I'll never be able to get out of my mind how beautiful Raven is today. A picture could never compare to her real beauty or be able to capture her heart and soul."

My mom was stunned. She put her hand over her mouth like she was watching a made-for-TV movie unfold in her very own living room. "You are making me misty-eyed."

"We have to go," I finally said.

"We have dinner reservations," Alexander stated proudly.

"Really?" my mother remarked. "Where?"

"It's a surprise," Alexander answered sweetly.

Billy Boy sauntered down the stairs and sized up my Victorian garb. "For a vampire, you look awesome," he commented.

"You say the most wonderful things!" I hugged my bewildered brother and my gushing parents. Then Alexander and I flew out the door.

* * *

"Are we going to Hatsy's Diner?" I asked as we drove toward town.

Alexander continued to drive in silence as I tried to guess where he was taking me. Finally he parked in front of Dullsville's cemetery.

"Old Jim, the caretaker, is at Lefty's Tavern for the night," he stated knowingly. "No one will bother us, except for the occasional mischievous ghost."

Alexander led me by the hand between the tombstones to the back end of the cemetery. A weeping willow was draped with its branches over a rectangular wooden table covered with a black lace tablecloth and set for two with fina china and sterling silverware.

Alexander lit the antique candelabra and politely held my chair out for me.

Beside each plate was a covered dish. The setting was beautifully morose. I wondered what the main course could be. I'd watched way too many horror films and I imagined opening the aluminum covers to find severed heads. However, when Alexander lifted them, a delicious sight and smell lay before us—a dinner of lemon chicken, buttered green beans, and rice pilaf.

Alexander poured us sparkling cherry wine in pewter goblets.

"This is way better than the Cricket Club," I said.

"To us," he said as we toasted our goblets.

The sparkling wine tickled my tongue, and Alexander and I began our meal.

"Just when I thought you'd outdone yourself at the cave, you present me a five-star dinner at a cemetery."

I gazed across the table, the candlelight glowing against Alexander's pale skin, highlighting his dark, mysterious eyes and sweet smile.

I had to pinch my arm to remind myself that this amazing and unusual romantic dinner with a vampire was undoubtedly real.

As Alexander drove through Dullsville High's parking lot, I couldn't believe my eyes. A half-dozen white limousines were lined up at the school's front entrance, dropping off groups of Dullsvillian teenagers as if they were movie stars. Next to the white stretches, Jameson's black Mercedes looked like a hearse.

From one limo emerged some of the soccer team members. A handsome Matt Wells extended his hand and helped my best friend, Becky, ease out of the elongated car.

At the head of the monstrous limo line, out popped Trevor and Jennifer Warren. As if it wasn't costly enough to arrive in a limousine, Trevor had a stretch for just the two of them.

Alexander pulled over and, ever the consummate gentleman, helped me out of the car. While he parked the Mercedes, I admired the red, white, and pink balloons tied by red ribbon to the railings of the gymnasium entrance.

My heart melted again when I saw Alexander in his silky black suit walking up the sidewalk of my school toward me.

There were so many students going in the main entrance, Alexander held back. Though he was glad to be going, I could tell he was equally overwhelmed in his new surroundings. He wasn't used to so many people in such a small area, fussing and flashing pictures.

I pulled him away from the crowd just to be sure he'd be safe from the cameras.

"Let's go through here," I said, stepping out of the crowded line.

We started for the side door, which was not being used.

As we walked through the corridors, Alexander studied everything—the trophy case, a display of yearbooks past, a bulletin board of weekly announcements. The mundane things I passed by on a daily basis and didn't even notice were like fascinating artifacts to my boyfriend.

"It's like a museum," he said.

"A boring one, right?"

"No, it helps me understand you more."

I gazed up at Alexander and squeezed his hand.

As we headed for the gymnasium, we passed giggling girls in gowns running to the bathroom to touch up their makeup and gossip about their dates—or possibly us.

Suddenly Alexander stopped. "Can we see your locker? I want to know as much as I can about how you spend your day."

"My locker?" I asked. "It's just a junky aluminum closet."

"But it's *your* junk," he said in a velvety voice. "I want to know everything about you."

His comment took my breath away. I held his hand in mine. "It's back this way."

We walked past the auditorium and biology and chemistry labs.

I spun the dial back and forth to the unlocking coordinates and opened my locker.

I was stunned. There, hanging on my door and filling the thin locker walls, were tiny painted portraits of Alexander and me. One of us in front of Hatsy's Diner, one dancing at Dullsville's golf course, and one designed with four vertical poses, as if it were a strip from a photo booth.

"These are amazing!"

Alexander beamed as one by one I viewed his astounding works of art.

"How did you get in here? I thought I was the only one who liked to sneak into places."

"I've been trying to give these to you since the cave. But I think this worked out better."

"I love them!"

"Now you can always see us together—and be like all the other girls with normal boyfriends."

I gave Alexander a huge hug and kissed him tenderly.

"I don't want a normal boyfriend."

He pushed my hair off my shoulder.

"I don't want to leave them," I said of my prized possessions. "I want to stare at them forever."

"Well, the real thing will have to do for tonight," he said, taking the picture of us on the golf course from my hand and tacking it back on my locker door. "I can hear the music starting."

I shut the door on my picture shrine, and Alexander

and I eagerly made our way to the gymnasium.

In bold letters above the gymnasium door hung a sign that read VIVA LAS VALENTINES. Red and white Mylar balloons and bright candy-colored streamers hung down over the entranceway like a beaded curtain. Dozens of Dullsville's decked-out students were mingling and filing into prom. I opened my silver chain-link purse and handed our tickets to an attending chaperone. I looked up. It was my study hall teacher, Mr. Ferguson.

"I see you finally came back," he said sternly, referring to my not returning to study hall.

"There was a long line at the water fountain."

Mr. Ferguson studied Alexander as we quickly filed past him and made our way into the gymnasium turned ballroom.

While the Snow Ball was elegant with its winter theme, the Prom Decorating Committee had outdone itself. Gigantic Necco-like candied paper hearts hung from the rafters like sugarcoated snowflakes. Phrases like BE MINE, TRUE LOVE, LET'S KISS, BE GOOD, SWEET TALK, and MY LOVE—in baby blue, Barbie pink, sunflower yellow, winter white, lavender lilac, and mermaid green danced within arms' reach in the air above us. The white gymnasium walls, normally covered with Dullsville High banners, were replaced with three-foot-high cupid cutouts and pink hearts. The hardwood basketball floors were sprinkled with red and white heart-shaped confetti. In one corner, a photographer was stationed to snap pictures of gown- and tuxedo-clad students with a giant red heart and white lacy valentine as a backdrop.

The band the Caped Crusaders, four men in their thirties wearing trendy black suits with cupid wings and white tennis shoes, were jamming on a makeshift stage underneath the home team's basket.

Dullsville's students had metamorphosed from cheerleaders and jocks into princesses and princes. Girls glistened in their evening gowns—a rainbow of pink, blue, red, and orange dresses from Jack's department store swept over the basketball court as if we were at a Hollywood premiere.

I noticed a small brunette girl in an amazing blue vintage gown holding the hand of her dashing young date.

"Becky!" I called, running over to her.

"Raven! I rode in a limousine!"

"I know. I saw you get out. You looked like a movie star!"

"You are the prettiest one here!" she gloated.

"No way, you are! That dress is so you—and so gorgeous!"

While Becky and I gushed, Alexander and Matt made small talk.

"Let's get our picture taken," Becky said. "All four of us."

My heart sank. Again I would have to miss pictures with Alexander.

"I'm still blinded from all the flashes at home," I said.

"Very funny." Becky pulled my arm and eagerly led me to the photo area. I glanced back. Matt was following us, but my dark-suited boyfriend stayed still.

"Where's Alexander?" Matt asked. "I thought he was right behind me."

"He hates pictures. Something about them stealing your soul," I rambled on.

A crowd of promgoers gathered, waiting for their Kodak moment. All of a sudden, Becky pulled Alexander from between a group of couples standing behind us.

"Your turn," the photographer said, pointing to me.

I froze, but Becky pulled me to the black duct-taped X marked on the center of the floor. "I'll cherish this forever.

"Maybe they'll pick this one for the yearbook," she continued.

"We can only hope," I said through a cheesy grin.

"I didn't know vampires showed up on film," I heard one of the students say. They were referring to me.

The photographer angled Becky and me in a V shape and arranged Matt and Alexander behind us as if they were giant game pieces.

I glanced back at Alexander, who I was surprised to find smiling for the camera.

"On the count of three," the photographer said. "One, two—"

"Hachoo!" I said, faking a sneeze.

"Bless you," my friends said.

"Gesundheit," the photographer said, stepping away from his digital camera. "Again, on the count of three." He focused behind the camera. "One, two—"

"I really must get a tissue," I said, holding my hand up.

Becky held my arm so I couldn't move.

"I have three hundred pictures to take this evening. I can't take the picture if you keep moving," the photographer warned.

I could feel the crowd around us getting restless.

The photographer stepped behind the camera.

"One—" The flash went off. Tricky man. Luckily the room was bright enough that the flash didn't blind me, much less Alexander.

Another couple scurried toward us, making their way for our spots.

"I'm thirsty," Alexander said anxiously, suddenly leading me through the crowd and away from the photographer.

As Alexander and I made our escape, I could hear Matt calling us.

"We have to take it again," he said. "The photographer cut Alexander out of the picture."

My nonphotographic boyfriend and I gathered at the punch bowl. The refreshment table was sprinkled with red and white chocolate kisses, bowls of Red Hots, and heart-shaped boxes filled with more chocolates.

I saw Jennifer Warren in the black cocktail dress I had wanted to purchase at Jack's. I was still annoyed she had pulled the dress out from under my nose, but she really did fill out the dress so beautifully that I couldn't help but tell her so.

"That dress was made for you."

"And yours as well," she said with a catlike grin.

"Thanks," I replied.

Deep down I knew she didn't mean it as a compliment.

Trevor, in an unbuttoned sleek black tux, crisp white shirt, and solid red silk tie, walked over to Jennifer.

He looked me over from my midnight black hair to my charcoal witchy boots.

"Too bad you didn't want that dance," he said softly. "I was planning on showing you a night to remember."

"It will be a night to remember. Only I'll be forgetting you were in it."

Just then, Alexander stepped between us. The Caped Crusaders began to play "Love Shack."

"May I have this dance?" Alexander said, offering his hand.

We left Trevor by the refreshments and for the next hour, Alexander and I rocked and rolled until I was seeing hearts. Finally we were both so exhausted, we headed back to the punch bowl for a pick-me-up.

Mr. Ferguson took center stage and stood in front of the Caped Crusaders. "I'd like to thank you all for coming out tonight for Viva las Valentines!" he said into the microphone to massive applause. "I'd like to thank the Decorating Committee for volunteering their time and transforming the gymnasium into a valentine paradise."

"Go, Becky!" I shouted, clapping for my best friend who was standing next to me.

"And finally to Shirley's Bakery for the candies and refreshments," Mr. Ferguson continued.

"Now we're applauding the punch bowl," I whispered to Alexander.

"I am very pleased to announce tonight's King and Queen."

"Woohoo!" a soccer snob shouted over the sound of applause.

"Drumroll, please . . . ," Mr. Ferguson commanded.

The crowd stood quiet as my study hall teacher opened a letter-sized valentine.

"I'd like to present to you this year's Prom King . . . Trevor Mitchell."

Trevor high-fived his soccer-snob teammates and ran up onstage like he was receiving the World Cup.

I rolled my eyes. "Big surprise. When Daddy owns all the land in Dullsville," I whispered to Alexander, "he can afford to buy his son a throne."

Heather came over to Trevor, who was now standing center stage, waving to the crowd, and placed a silver staff in his hand and a crown on top of his blond locks.

"And this year's prom queen . . ." Mr. Ferguson opened the second valentine and began to say, "Jen—"

Jennifer Warren started for the aisle.

Mr. Ferguson's eyes bulged out like Jameson's. He cleared his throat and said, "I mean, Raven Madison."

The crowd went quiet.

"Raven Madison," he said again.

I stared at Trevor, who gave me a triumphant wink.

All eyes were on me as the spotlight hit my face.

"This must be wrong," I said to Alexander.

Jennifer Warren stood stunned at the foot of the stage. "This is my senior year! I demand a recount!"

Becky started clapping. "Raven, Raven!" The other promgoers were as shocked as I was, but they joined her.

"Raven! Raven! Raven!" the crowd began to cheer.

"Get up there," Becky said, pushing me toward the stage.

I gathered my dress and walked up the few stairs toward the stage. It felt like an eternity, walking in slow motion, as I headed over to Trevor and Mr. Ferguson. Heather came over, gave me an evil look, put a silver faux-diamond-encrusted tiara on my head, and handed me a bouquet of red roses.

I awkwardly smiled as the crowd cheered. I felt like I was in a scene from *Carrie*. I now knew what my payback from Trevor would be. He'd imagined that I'd be excited that I, the school oddball, had been chosen by the student body to be Prom Queen. At any moment, just like in the horror film, a bucket of pig's blood would fall on me, embarrassing and belittling me in front of the whole school.

Only I had a different weapon than Carrie had.

A Victorian parasol.

I opened my elegant umbrella and glared back at Trevor, then the crowd.

I waited. And waited. And waited.

Nothing came down. Not even heart-shaped confetti from the ceiling.

I stared out into the crowd of Dullsville High faces, all looking confused. Then it hit me and I realized my fate.

Trevor had a far worse plan for me than embarrassing

me with pig's blood—he wanted to dance with me in front of the whole school and, most important, Alexander.

"This dance belongs to Prom King and Queen, Trevor Mitchell and Raven Madison," Mr. Ferguson announced.

All eyes were on me. I wanted to run, but I was surrounded by staring students.

Trevor gripped my hand harder than a goalie holding a soccer ball.

I saw Alexander, who stared back at me, his eyes lonely, clapping with the rest of the students. I felt awful holding another guy's hand in front of Alexander, especially the hand of my nemesis.

Trevor led me down the steps of the stage and pulled me onto the center of the dance floor.

The lights dimmed, and red hearts danced around the gymnasium walls and floor.

I could barely breathe. Trevor put his arm around my waist and pulled me close.

I was dizzy from the lights and the music. I felt sick to my stomach. I didn't invite Alexander to come with me to prom to watch me dance with Trevor Mitchell.

I didn't care what prom protocol dictated or who Trevor had paid off.

I pulled away from my nemesis. "You fixed this," I yelled over the music. "I'm not really Prom Queen. This dance belongs to Jennifer Warren."

"Don't ditch me in front of the whole school," Trevor said through gritted teeth, trying to grasp my hand back.

"Forget it!"

"Once a freak, always a freak. I'll get you, Monster Girl."

Trevor's words churned through my veins like jagged glass. As far as Trevor and I'd come in the last few weeks, we were right back to being two kids in kindergarten.

I pulled my tiara off my head.

Jennifer, who was being consoled by the Prada shoe snob, smiled at me.

"This belongs to you." I handed her my tiara.

I turned around, triumphant, to celebrate with my vampire boyfriend.

Instead, all the smiling faces I saw were mortal.

I looked everywhere, making myself dizzy searching for Alexander in the sea of promgoers as they watched Trevor and Jennifer Warren dance. It took me a moment to catch my breath, my heart was beating so fast. I pushed through the crowd and found Becky and Matt. "Where is Alexander?"

"I don't know. He was here a minute ago. I can't believe you are Prom Queen! Why did you give your tiara to Jennifer?"

"We'll talk later. I have to find Alexander."

"Hey—we have to retake the picture of us," Matt called to me.

I searched the tables where couples were sitting. Not a vampire among them.

"Have you seen Alexander?" I asked our class treasurer.

"Who's Alexander?"

I ran over to the punch table. A few couples were munching on chocolate kisses.

"Have any of you seen Alexander?"

"Alexander who?" one kid answered. "The zombie? I think he's already been buried."

My heart sank.

I raced to the side exit. A sign read EMERGENCY USE ONLY. IF DOOR IS OPENED, ALARM WILL SOUND.

Drats!

I passed the photographer, who was dismantling his equipment. I flew out the gymnasium entrance and hurried down the hallway.

Memories of the nightmarish end to the Snow Ball came storming back to me. Running outside in the pouring rain, finding a lone Alexander, begging him to talk to me as he walked home to the Mansion.

However, when I opened Dullsville High's main door, it wasn't pouring rain—or raining at all—but was cool and quiet.

"Alexander!" I called.

There, standing at the bottom of the stairs with his back toward me, was my vampire boyfriend.

I gathered the hem of my dress and hurried down the front steps.

"Alexander, please. I didn't want to dance with that jerk."

Alexander didn't reply.

"Please, look at me," I said, my eyes welling with tears.

Alexander turned to me and stepped aside, revealing Henry, who was standing with him.

The pit of my stomach turned. What was Henry doing at prom?

"Where's Billy Boy?" I asked, worried.

"He just told me he was going to Valentine's house," Henry said.

"He's supposed to be grounded," I said.

"I thought you should know."

I gazed at Alexander, who seemed as surprised to find Henry here as I was.

"Valentine said he'd been staying with his aunt, Maria Maxwell," Billy's nerd-mate continued. "Since Billy's been grounded, I had some free time, so I searched the town records for Valentine's aunt. I couldn't find her listed anywhere. There is not a trace of anyone here by that name. Then, tonight, Billy dropped off our Project Vampire for me to work on. I found this."

Henry handed Alexander an eight-by-ten weathered piece of parchment paper.

It was a gravestone etching.

In jagged letters were the words:

Maria Maxwell
Beloved Aunt
1824–1922

16

Sibling Rivalry

I have to find Billy before it's too late," said Alexander. "Valentine is at the end of his rope. If I don't return within an hour, have Matt drive you home." Alexander gave me a quick kiss on the cheek and started toward his car.

"I'm going with you," I said, following after him.

"Stay here," he said, proceeding on. "I'll come back for you when I'm finished."

"I'm coming too. Billy's my brother."

Alexander continued cutting through the grass instead of walking on the sidewalk.

"Where does Maria Maxwell live?" I asked. "Or, I mean, where's she buried? In Dullsville's cemetery?"

"Henry said Billy was going to Valentine's house. I have an idea where that might be."

When Alexander and I reached the Mercedes, my usually gentlemanly boyfriend didn't open the door for me. Alexander was preoccupied as he started the car. We continued to sit in silence as we drove through downtown.

"This isn't how I imagined spending my prom," I said. "Trevor getting even with me and now Billy Boy in harm's way."

"Trevor is more of a vampire than I am," Alexander admitted. "He thinks like one and acts like one."

"That's why I love you," I said. "You are a vampire with a soul."

"While I am buried in the darkness of my coffin, I know Trevor can see you every day, share classes with you, gaze at you in the cafeteria. Things I never get to do—and will never be able to do. I know he was shoving it in my face."

"Well, it's a heavenly face," I said, caressing his shoulder.

"You looked so beautiful tonight," Alexander said as he continued to drive. "I only wish I could have been the Prom King dancing with you."

"Well, I didn't dance with Trevor. I gave the tiara to Jennifer Warren. She's the most popular girl in school. I can guarantee, now that Trevor tricked both me *and* her, he'll be riding home tonight in his million-dollar stretch limo alone."

I gazed out into darkness and at the same haze-covered fields we passed a few days ago. We drove through a forgotten meadow and along a bumpy dirt path.

The car's headlights shined on the darkened cavern and illuminated something shiny at the mouth of the cave.

I quickly got out of the car. Billy Boy's bike was outside.

"You were right!" I said proudly. "My brother's here."

Alexander handed me the flashlight and we crept into the darkened cave.

"Billy!" I called, but only my voice echoed back to me.

A few inches of water trickled over the stone floor as we traipsed through the dark and dank cave in our prom outfits. I held the hem of my dress up with one hand and the flashlight with the other while Alexander kindly guided me through our subterranean surroundings.

"This isn't like Billy. He's not this adventurous. This is something I'd do."

"Maybe that's why he's doing it," Alexander deduced. "To be more like you."

"I thought he was trying to impress Valentine."

"Maybe impressing you is more important to him."

"Billy!" I called. No answer.

We reached the trickling waterfall and fanglike stalactites where Alexander and I had had our romantic interlude. Alexander and I stopped and called out to Billy again. Once again we didn't hear an answer.

My flashlight illuminated what seemed to be a round patch on the stone floor. On further inspection, I realized it was a circle of dirt.

"This circle isn't big enough for a coffin," I stated.

"He's not sleeping in a coffin," Alexander surmised. He pointed above us. I turned my light toward the cave's ceiling. A few bats, hanging upside down, were startled and flew off.

I gasped. "Is one of them Valentine?"

Alexander shook his head.

We continued to forge on, proceeding farther into the cave than we'd explored the last time we were here.

"Billy!" Alexander hollered.

My light caught an odd shape in front of us. At first it appeared to be a dead end. But then I realized the cave split off in two different directions.

"Which way do we go?" I asked anxiously.

"We'll have to separate," Alexander instructed. "We don't have enough time to search each path together. I'll be able to find you."

But will we be able to find Billy? I wondered.

Alexander squeezed my hand and then let go. I flashed the light in his direction, but he was gone.

I shined my light in front of me. A chill ran through my veins. The air was cool and smelled musty. I took a deep breath and proceeded into the passageway. As I journeyed deeper into the cave, the passageway narrowed, the walls closing in on me. Soon the branch of the cave was only wide enough for one person to fit through.

Normally I'd have been exhilarated, feeling comforted by the nocturnal elements around me. Instead I was anxious. If I didn't get to Billy Boy in time, he'd be grounded for eternity.

As I crept through the skinny passageway, the air turned chillier and the sound of trickling water grew faint. The flashlight illuminated only a small pathway before me. I averted any protruding stalagmites by reaching out before me in the blinding darkness as I continued on my way, deeper into the cave.

"Billy!" I shouted. "Billy—where are you?"

The narrow walls of the passageway suddenly opened. In the distance, I saw what appeared to be flickering lights a few yards away. Maybe Billy was flashing an SOS. I gathered the hem of my dress and hurried toward the light.

It was a lit candelabra.

"Billy!" I pointed the flashlight everywhere—the moss-carpeted walls, the rock-encrusted floor, the mile-high ceiling.

Suddenly I felt a presence standing next to me. I shined the light on the figure.

It was Billy Boy.

"Billy!" I exclaimed. I reached out and hugged my startled brother.

"What are you doing here?" he asked, surprised.

"I should be asking you that!"

I quickly checked my brother's neck for any bite marks.

"What are you doing?"

"I just wanted to make sure you are okay."

"I'm fine. Don't tell Mom. I'll be grounded again. Valentine wanted to show me this cave before he finally took me to the place where he's been staying."

This is where he's been staying! I almost said.

"We came here to get more samples for our vampire project," Billy Boy said proudly.

You're the vampire project, I wanted to tell him.

"Promise you won't snitch on Valentine. He's from Romania and knows a lot about the history of vampires, caves, and bats."

"But you're terrified of bats!"

"Shh!" he whispered. "Swear you won't tell him."

"I swear. Now let's go—"

"Valentine was just here," Billy Boy said, glancing around. "We were going to meet his aunt."

"You want to meet his aunt?" I asked. "This is Valentine's aunt."

I handed my brother Jagger's gravestone etching.

Billy Boy gasped, his face turning as white as a corpse. "But she's . . ."

"I know. I warned you about Valentine. Hurry, we have to go."

"Why would Valentine lie? Where is he?" he said, concerned. "We can't leave him—"

"Alexander will take care of him. You and I have to leave."

"I have to grab my backpack. Our project is inside it."

"Forget about your—"

Before I could finish my sentence, my brother had already taken off.

Valentine stepped out of the shadows.

Weakened and wearied, Valentine appeared more deathly than ever, as if he'd been lying at the bottom of a frozen lake. His lips were ice blue and his teeth were chattering, but that didn't stop the devilish boy from inching closer.

"Where's Billy!" I demanded.

"More important, where are *my* siblings?"

"I don't know. I already explained before that I thought they went back to Romania."

"Well, they didn't. Something—or someone—kept them from returning," he said accusingly.

"Is that why you were reading Billy's, Trevor's, and my thoughts? To find Jagger and Luna?"

"Yes, but I read a lot more than I imagined."

"What do you mean?"

Valentine inched closer.

"When I read Trevor's blood, I saw a covenant by the graveyard with Grim Reapers all around. A girl in a tattered prom dress walked up the aisle. But when she lifted her veil, instead of seeing my sister's face—I saw yours."

"You are talking about the Graveyard Gala—Trevor's party at the cemetery. That's not how it happened."

"I know, but that's how Trevor wanted it to happen. He never wanted my sister; he settled for her because she reminded him of you."

"I don't believe it."

"My family has been shamed ever since Alexander ditched my sister in Romania. Jagger came here to seek his revenge on that cowardly vampire. Then he called for my sister. Only they never called for me—because they think I'm a kid."

"That's normal. Billy feels left out all the time," I tried to assure him.

"But now that I'm here, I see that you are the cause of

them being shamed again," Valentine said, advancing toward me. "Now they won't ever return to me and my family. Neither Trevor nor Alexander wanted my sister. They both want you—and they still do."

"I don't know what you mean. Why would Alexander 'still' want me—he already has me."

"Not completely. Remember . . . Alexander is a vampire, after all," Valentine said, and flashed his fangs.

I paused.

"I've read his blood. He's hungered for your flesh, blood, and soul since he laid eyes on you."

"I don't care what you say; you are just trying to destroy our relationship. But you can't!"

"Or can I? How long can you two be together when one craves the blood of the other? How long will you torment him? For eternity?"

"Maybe I'm the one who's tormented. I want to be in Alexander's world and he wants to protect me from it—and vampires like you!"

"Valentine—you've said enough!" I heard a familiar voice say.

I turned around. Alexander was standing behind me.

I gazed up at Alexander's dark eyes. Were Valentine's words about my boyfriend correct? Alexander backed away from me.

"Valentine—you have to leave this cave and this town now," I demanded.

"I won't leave until I've gotten what I came here for. And since I can't find my brother, I'll have to take yours."

Out of the darkness, Billy Boy traipsed toward me, his backpack slung over his shoulder.

Valentine grabbed my brother's puny arm and lifted his wrist to his mouth.

"What are you doing?" Billy Boy asked.

Valentine smiled a wicked grin and flashed his fangs.

"No!" I cried.

Valentine opened his mouth wide and began to bear down on my brother's wrist.

I shined the flashlight on Valentine's face. His green eyes turned crystal white, then bloodred.

Valentine let out a horrible yell and withdrew his grip from my brother's wrist. He covered his face from the light and recoiled into the shadows.

Valentine lay in the cave, appearing more ghastly than ever, his lips blue and his skin paler than a corpse's.

"Valentine's not moving," I said. "I think I . . ."

Alexander scooped the limp vampire up in his arms. Billy Boy was visibly shaken. I held his trembling hand and led him back through the cave.

When we reached the entrance, Billy grabbed his bike while Alexander and I put Valentine in the car.

As Alexander laid the weary Valentine on the backseat, the preteen vampire struggled to open his eyes.

"I tried," Valentine whispered to Alexander, "but I couldn't do it."

"Try to save your breath," Alexander warned.

Valentine clutched my boyfriend's arm. "When I spent the night at Billy's and read his blood in search of my siblings, I found out something else instead. Billy was peacefully dreaming about his family; his mother, father, and Raven. I couldn't take him away from that. Jagger and Luna were right to exclude me. I am not like them after all."

Alexander placed a warm blanket around the boy and I sat with him as he laid down, his breathing labored.

Billy Boy disassembled the front wheel from his bike, and Alexander helped place it in the trunk. I joined my brother in the passenger seat of the Mercedes.

"I got you this," Billy Boy said, handing me a bat-shaped rock he'd found in the cave. "I thought you'd think it was cool."

Mortal or vampire, Valentine and Billy Boy were just like any other boys their age—desperately fighting to be seen by their older siblings as anything but a child.

When Alexander, Billy Boy, Valentine, and I arrived back at Benson Hill, Henry was waiting for us on the uneven steps of the Mansion.

As if on cue, Jameson opened the heavy Mansion door. Alexander carried Valentine up the grand staircase as the nerd-mates and I followed into the foyer.

"Wow! This place is huge!" Henry exclaimed.

"And spooky. There must be dozens of ghosts in here," my brother added.

Jameson directed Henry, Billy Boy, and me to wait in the parlor while the creepy man busied himself in the kitchen.

The parlor was the same as always—a simple desk, a

shelf of dusty books, and a few antique Victorian chairs.

"There isn't much to look at in here besides dust," Henry observed. "I'd love to take a tour of the Mansion."

"That isn't possible right now."

My brother plopped in a chair while Henry opened a few ancient books that didn't appear to have been touched since the Mansion had been built.

"Why isn't Alexander taking him to a doctor?" Billy Boy asked.

"It's hard to explain," I answered.

"Henry and I are members of the chess, math, and astronomy clubs. I think if it's a concept you understand, we can comprehend it too."

I groaned. "Alexander can help Valentine out more than a doctor can. It's something about being from Romania."

Jameson, carrying a tray of bottles filled with red liquid, hurried up the grand staircase.

The boys looked at each other incredulously.

"Are you thinking what I'm thinking?" Billy Boy asked Henry.

"I'm surprised we didn't figure it out sooner," the nerd-mate replied.

"We were looking at the wrong subject!" Billy Boy said. "Now it all makes sense."

"Not only will we get an A," Henry concluded, "but we may get a scholarship to MIT."

"What are you two talking about?" I asked.

"Our subject for Project Vampire," Henry replied matter-of-factly. "He's lying upstairs."

"Are you crazy?" I asked.

The two boys pulled their chairs toward mine and leaned in to me like they were about to divulge a major secret.

"The truth lies in the proof," Billy Boy pronounced. "One, I saw a green-eyed bat hanging outside my room. Valentine has green eyes."

"Two," Henry chimed in. "Valentine was looking for my treehouse. Then one day, hanging on a limb we found blood-filled amulets."

"Three," Billy Boy added. "Valentine is from Romania."

"Four, he was living in a cave."

"Five," my brother continued. "Valentine's deathly allergic to garlic."

"Six," Henry added. "He tried to have us become blood brothers."

"Seven, he tried to bite me," Billy Boy argued.

"I tried to bite you last year!" I countered.

Billy Boy stopped and geared up for his verdict. "We think Valentine is a vampire."

"That project has gone to your head." I laughed.

"Then this won't matter," my brother challenged, extending his hand toward his nerd-mate's backpack. "Henry . . ."

The wunderkind unzipped his navy blue sack. He held out a small rectangular mirror.

"When Valentine comes down," Billy Boy said, "then we'll see. Or we'll observe what we don't see."

The boys stared at me proudly like two nerdy Sherlock Holmeses.

I was floored. Billy and Henry, the nerd-mate super-sleuths, were on the cusp of proving that Valentine was indeed a real vampire.

I'd been spending the last few weeks trying to keep Valentine away from the boys for their protection. Now I'd have to keep the nerd-mates away from Valentine and Alexander—for the vampires' safety.

"Why don't we take a look around this mansion," Henry said, rising.

"Why don't we not," I ordered, pointing to the Victorian chair. "Here—read this," I said, handing him a fifty-pound book on Stonehenge, pyramids, and UFOs. "Maybe this will help you conclude that Valentine is an alien."

After the boys exhausted themselves by perusing old dusty books, Henry busied himself playing games on his cell phone.

"In the cave," my brother began, "I heard you call me Billy. Not Nerd Boy. Not Billy Boy."

"So, what of it?"

"I know you are capable of calling me by my real name."

"Your real name is William. Is that what you want me to call you?"

"How about plain old 'Billy.'"

"Fine. From now on," I said, "it's 'Plain Old Billy.'"

My brother wrinkled his nose at me, then shook his

head. "My turn," he said, reaching for Henry's phone.

The two boys watched *Star Trek* on Henry's cell while I peered out the window into the moonlit night. I began to piece together Valentine's motive for arriving in Dullsville.

According to Valentine, he turned up in town to look for his siblings. He'd been hoping to find Jagger and Luna still there. When Valentine found it empty of coffins, he searched the treehouse for clues to their whereabouts.

There Valentine must have found Jagger's hidden tombstone etchings that I had come across earlier. But what was it about the etchings that would provide a clue to Jagger and Luna's location?

I remembered Valentine and Billy Boy holding them when I discovered Valentine in my brother's room.

"Billy, didn't you and Valentine search the Internet for the location of Valentine's gravestone etchings?" I asked.

"Yes, one was from Romania and one from the cemetery here in town, but not the one you showed me in the cave. You busted into my bedroom when we were about to do a search. Why?"

Instead of answering, I turned to my brother's nerdmate. "Henry—does your cell phone log on to the Internet?"

The geeky techno wizard rolled his eyes like I was so yesterday.

"Just for kicks," I began, "would you search for the name Maria Maxwell?"

Henry quickly got online and tapped in the name of Valentine's great aunt to the hundredth degree.

I waited for the cybergeek's response.

"There is a Dr. Maria Maxwell in Spokane. She has a Web site. Do you want to look?"

"Any other listings?" I asked.

"A Maria Maxwell completed the Chicago Marathon in October 2001."

"Too young."

"A Maria Maxwell who wrote a children's book."

"In 1800?"

"No, in 1976."

"Try using the birth date we found on the etching. Maybe she's buried in a small town in Romania."

"Maria Maxwell," he said as he typed. "1844."

We waited for a moment, but it seemed like an eternity. The *tick tock* of the grandfather clock looming in the hallway loudly drummed to the throbbing rhythm of my own heartbeat.

"Here is a link for the standard news archives— obituaries—nineteen twenty-two—"

"Let me see," I said anxiously.

Henry angled the phone so we could both read the tiny screen.

It read: "Maria Maxwell. Born in the small town of Sighisoara, Romania. Immigrated to America and settled in Greenville Village, where she lived out her ninety-eight years. Loved by all. Beloved aunt to ten nieces and nephews, all of whom remain in Romania."

"Where is Greenville Village?" I wondered aloud.

"Scroll up to the city's newspaper."

Then Henry showed me, plain as day on the small cell phone screen.

It was the Hipsterville *Ledger*.

Finally, I heard the morbidly slow shuffling of Jameson's footsteps plodding down the grand staircase. I caught up to the butler in the hallway on his way to check in on us in the parlor.

"How is Valentine?" I asked the creepy man.

"He's coming along, Miss Raven. I gave him some Romanian smoothies. Alexander is attending to him. How are you and the boys?"

Henry and my brother poked their heads out the parlor doorway.

"We're fine."

"Can I use your phone?" I asked.

"Of course you may. There is one in the study."

I didn't want to use Henry's cell and have any traces of my call linked to his phone. The boys were on to Valentine's identity enough as it was without my help.

"Would you boys like some smoothies?" Jameson asked politely as he headed for the parlor.

All I could think of were the bloodred Romanian smoothies I saw him carrying up to Valentine. "Make them American ones," I suggested seriously.

The nerd-mates eagerly followed Jameson into the kitchen, eyeing the portraits and lit candles in the hallway.

Once in the study, I found an antique phone sitting on a grand oakwood desk. I picked up the heavy black phone, which had a cord and dials instead of push buttons and a battery.

I stuck my index finger into the round number one, steered it to the right, and let go, then watched it dial back. I had only nine more numbers to go.

My finger shook as I continued to dial.

The phone connected and the other line began to ring. And ring. And ring.

C'mon, pick up!

The other end answered. I could hear the gothic-rock pulsating sounds of the Caretakers.

"Coffin Club. Romeo speaking."

I paused and took a deep breath.

"Romeo? Is Jagger there?"

There was silence on the other end. I was certain Romeo would say no or, worse, hang up.

"Jagger just left. He should be back in an hour," he replied.

I'd found Jagger! I couldn't believe it! Valentine was right—Jagger hadn't returned to Romania.

"May I ask who's calling?" Romeo continued.

"Yes," I answered, then said, "tell him it's his aunt Maria."

18

Final Farewell

Henry and Billy Boy were playing chess on Henry's cell phone and I was leafing through *Historical Romania* when a haggard Alexander finally appeared in the drawing room, minus his prom suit jacket.

I raced over to my worn-out boyfriend.

"How is Valentine?" I asked.

"He's resting," he assured me, placing his hand on my shoulder.

"And you?"

"I'm fine," he said, relieved.

"Is he all right?" Billy Boy inquired.

"Yes," Alexander replied. "We reached him in time."

"What was wrong with him?" Henry asked.

"He was dehydrated. Jameson whipped up some smoothies and now he's rejuvenated."

The boys eagerly eyed each other.

"Can we see him?" Billy Boy asked.

Henry held the mirror in his hand. "Yes. We'd like to take a look at him."

I gave Alexander a knowing glance. "The boys think Valentine is a vampire."

Henry and Billy Boy appeared embarrassed.

"Maybe you guys are getting dehydrated too," Alexander mused.

"We shouldn't disturb him," my boyfriend continued. "But he wanted me to tell you both he said thank you."

"We'd really like to see him," Henry insisted.

"It's getting late," I stated. "Billy was already grounded once this week."

"Jameson will take you all home," Alexander said.

"Cool!" my brother said, and high-fived his friend.

I paused. Prom night was over? While the rest of Dullsville High partied into the wee hours, I was being sent home. I understood the nerd-mates needed to be tucked into bed, but me?

"All of us?" I tried to clarify.

While Billy Boy and Henry collected their things, Alexander pulled me to the side. He leaned against the grandfather clock.

"I'm sorry your prom night had to end this way."

"The night has just begun," I said.

"You are right. My night has just begun. Valentine can no longer search for Jagger and Luna on his own. I must find them for him. I've spent the last six months evading the Maxwells. It's ironic; now I'll be the one who's seeking them out."

"I think I know where Jagger and Luna are," I said proudly.

"You do?" he asked.

"Hipsterville."

"How do you know that?"

"That is where his aunt, Maria Maxwell, is buried. Henry and I searched on the Internet."

"But how do you know Jagger is there?"

"I checked. He was just hanging out at the Coffin Club."

"Then they are closer than I thought," he said, relieved. "That's great news."

As we reached the doorway, and the nerd-mates hopped down the front steps and out to Jameson's waiting car, I gazed up at the moon as it slowly became blanketed by a hazy cloud.

It hit me what Alexander had just revealed to me. He'd have to take Valentine to Hipsterville—now.

I knew I had a grave situation on my hands.

"When I come back tomorrow at sunset, you won't be here, will you?"

Alexander said nothing.

I turned and saw Billy Boy and Henry getting into Jameson's car.

My heart felt like a silver bullet had just penetrated it.

"You'll be leaving tonight . . . when Jameson returns."

Alexander didn't answer. Instead, he placed his hand on my shoulder.

"That's not fair. I don't want you to leave the Mansion again. Ever . . . ," I continued.

A tear welled up in my eye.

"How long will you be?" I asked.

"As long as it takes," he said, trying to comfort me, but his own dark eyes were sad.

"I can't be without you, not for a second, much less a sunset," I said, my heart breaking.

"Neither can I, but I have no choice. Valentine cannot stay here any longer, for his own safety, mine, and all of Dullsville's."

I knew what Alexander was doing had to be done. However, that didn't mean that I had to like it.

"Take me with you to Hipsterville. Then we won't be apart for a moment."

"You have school—"

"It's the weekend, and we have teachers' prep day next week. I can stay with my aunt Libby. I'm sure Jameson can convince my parents. He's very charming."

"I'll be going places that you shouldn't know about. Places that aren't safe for a mortal like you. It's best for both of us that I'm the one who leaves."

Leaves? I was crushed.

Then Valentine's own words earlier tonight in the cave about Alexander's innermost thoughts came back to me. Maybe by leaving, Alexander felt he was protecting me, too.

"This isn't about Valentine, is it?" I asked, my words breaking in my throat. "It's about what Valentine found out when he read your thoughts."

Alexander turned toward the moon.

My eyes filled with tears. I grasped his arm. "I'm happy to know that you thirst for me the same way I thirst for you. I want us to be together—in your world."

"I know, but—"

I put my finger on his lips.

"That's always been my dream. Since I was a little girl. My middle name is 'Vampire.'"

Alexander took my hand in his. "I never meant to put you in any danger—and that's all I've ever done since I met you. Valentine is right. I am a threat to you—on many levels."

"I've never felt threatened by you—only loved. You are no more a threat than Trevor."

"Trevor can't take you into the Underworld. And now that you know that I've struggled with . . . that I've even considered taking you there . . . ," Alexander said in a serious voice. "Now that I'll be leaving for Hipsterville, I can at least be assured that you will be safe—from the Maxwells and from me."

Alexander's sullen eyes turned even darker.

"You are going to take Valentine to Hipsterville and then never return," I said.

Alexander didn't reply.

"Then Valentine and Jagger have gotten their revenge! They've turned nothing more than rambling thoughts against us. They've gotten exactly what they wanted. They've destroyed you—and me!"

Tears streamed down my face.

I stood on the stairs, preparing to hear the door slam behind me.

Instead I heard nothing. But I felt the same familiar presence I'd felt behind me when I'd snuck into the Mansion. I felt a warm, gentle hand on my shoulder. I turned around and saw Alexander still standing there, a tear in his eye. My gothic guy, my vampire-mate. He stood before me like a knight of the night.

He took my hand in his and held it to his lips.

"Raven, you understand that I cannot survive without the darkness, blood, and my coffin."

"I know . . . ," I said, choking up.

"Since I've moved into the Mansion, I learned something."

"Yes?"

"I cannot survive without *you*."

I smiled through my own raining tears. I fell into his arms and wrapped my arms around his waist.

Alexander caressed my hair. I gazed up into his dark, mysterious eyes. He kissed me.

"Jameson is waiting," he said softly. "I'll be back before you even miss me."

"I miss you already."

It took all my strength to tear myself away from Alexander.

Tears dripped down my face as I ran toward the car, already feeling his absence. Alexander could be away for days, weeks, even months.

"Why are you crying?" Billy Boy asked when I hopped into the Mercedes. "You'll see him tomorrow."

I pressed my hand to the window. I could see Alexander standing on the Mansion steps, his hand also raised toward mine, his shadowy image getting smaller and smaller as Jameson drove us farther away from the Mansion.

The car pulled around the gate. I turned around. The Mansion door was closed.

Alexander was gone.

Acknowledgments

I am grateful to these amazing people—Katherine Tegen, my wonderful editor, for your friendship, talent, and making my dreams come true!

Ellen Levine, my fabulous agent, for your outstanding advice and continued guidance in my career.

Julie Lansky at HarperCollins, for your great suggestions and firsthand knowledge of marathons.

My father and mother, Gary and Suzanne Schreiber, for being the best parents in the world.

My brother, Ben, for your support and enthusiasm.

And Eddie Lerer, for being my Alexander.

Read on for a preview of the fifth book
in the sizzling Vampire Kisses series:

The Coffin Club

I flew from class like a bat out of hell.

Dullsville High's bell rang its final year-end ring and I was the first student to arrive at my locker. Normally the sound of the bell grated on my nerves like a woodpecker hammering on a sycamore, but this time the buzzing was as melodious as the sound of a harpsichord. It signaled one thing: summer vacation.

The two words rolled off my tongue like the sweet-tasting nectar of the blossoming honeysuckles. Aren't all vacations sweet? Given. However, summer vacation beats out its sister vacations—spring and winter break. Summer vacation surpasses them all with its incomparable advantages—two and a half months of freedom from textbooks, teachers, and torment. No detentions, lectures, or pop quizzes. No more spending an eight-hour day in the confines of Dullsville High, being the only goth in the preppy-filled school, or trying to lift an overslept pre-caffeinated head off my wooden desk. And most important, I could sleep in late. Just like a vampire.

My red and white school-colored handcuffs had been slipped off my wrists.

I was so pumped I even beat model student and my best friend, Becky, to her locker. It was the last time I'd have to remember, or forget, as I often did, the lock's random coordinates. Unreturned textbooks, notebooks, candy wrappers, and CDs filled the tiny metal closet. Forever the procrastinator, I waited until the final moment to clean it out. Unlike other lockers that had actual photographs of couples, staring back at me were oil-based pictures of me and Alexander that he'd painted and surprised me with, by hanging them in my locker. I gazed at them adoringly and carefully untacked one when I became distracted by the huge mess in front of me. I figured I needed a wheelbarrow to haul the load to Becky's truck but instead dragged out a dented garbage can and tossed out anything that I hadn't paid for.

"Summer's here! Can you believe it?" Becky said, catching up to me. We clasped hands and shrieked like we had just won tickets to a sold-out concert.

"It's finally here!" I exclaimed. "No more tardy slips or calls to my parents about dress codes."

Becky opened her locker, which had already been cleaned out. Photos of her and Matt presumably had been placed in a scrapbook with colorful captions, beautiful borders, and funky heart-shaped stickers. She examined the empty locker for anything else she might have forgotten.

"It looks like you even dusted it," I teased.

"This is going to be the best summer ever, Raven. This is the first summer we both will have boyfriends. To think, we'll be lying poolside with the hottest guys in Dullsville."

I spotted a painting of Alexander and me in front of Hatsy's Diner that still hung on the inside of my locker door. The stars twinkled above us and we were lit by the glow of the moon.

"Well, one of us will be," I said. And I wasn't referring to the fact that my boyfriend wouldn't be able to worship the sun.

I had a bigger problem—he wasn't even in Dullsville.

Becky must have read my wistful expression. "I bet Alexander will be back anytime now to have graveside picnics with you," Becky offered with a bright smile.

Alexander and his creepy-but-kind butler, Jameson, had driven the ailing tween vampire, Valentine Maxwell, to Hipsterville in hopes of reuniting him with his nefariously Draculine siblings, Jagger and Luna. After Valentine tried to sink his tiny fangs into my little brother, Billy Boy, my sibling and his best friend, Henry, began questioning his possible nocturnal identity. While Alexander was upstairs in his attic room saving the sickly boy with Jameson's Romanian concoctions, I figured out and confirmed Jagger's and Luna's location—the Coffin Club. And with that, Alexander was forced to leave me behind in Dullsville as he reunited Valentine with his older siblings.

Alexander had promised me that he would return to Dullsville shortly. However, what we thought would be an overnight visit to Hipsterville turned into two, then three days. Then longer.

The sultry homeschooled Romanian vampire Alexander had brought life into my already darkened one. As the lonely old Mansion remained empty of its unearthly inhabitants, I began to miss specific things about him—the way he softly brushed my hair away from my face or traced the lace of my skirt with his ghost white fingers. I missed his dreamy chocolate brown eyes, his bright, sexy smile, his tender lips pressed to mine.

I managed to remove myself as the third wheel from Matt and Becky's go-cart of fun. In the moonlit evenings, instead of reluctantly cheering on the school's soccer team, I often visited the empty Mansion, sitting beneath its skeletal trees, by its wrought-iron gates, or on its uneven weed-filled cracked cement front steps. Other times, I'd hang out in the gazebo where Alexander and I'd shared romantic desserts and stolen kisses.

I assured myself that at any moment I'd see the head-lights of Jameson's Mercedes beaming up the winding driveway, but every night I went home alone, the driveway devoid of any hearse-like vehicles.

I crossed each passing day off my Emily the Strange calendar with a giant black X. It was starting to look like a one-sided tic-tac-toe game. Occasionally the doorbell rang, and when it did, I'd race to the front door in wild expectation of Alexander wrapping his pale arms around me, scooping me up, and planting me with a passionate kiss. Instead of being greeted by my boyfriend, I was met by the Flower Power delivery woman holding a bouquet of roses. My already darkened bedroom was beginning to resemble Dullsville's funeral home.

With each passing day, I wondered what could be taking him so long. Was he once again protecting me from something dangerous and underworldly? My boyfriend, always shrouded in a bit of mystery, only made me love him more.

I had secured the painting of us in my backpack and then untacked a special item next to it—my Coffin Club barbed-wire bracelet.

The Coffin Club. The most gothically haunting nightspot in Hipsterville. I'd stumbled upon the hangout when I visited the funky town a few months ago. Unlike any other club I'd ever been to, the Coffin Club was the antithesis of Dullsville High. It was the first place where I really fit in, surrounded by similar taste, style, and attitude. I dreamed of returning there with Alexander on my arm. Only now I was miles away from my favorite nightclub and my favorite guy.

I untacked the painting of Alexander and me dancing at Dullsville's golf course.

I'd give anything to be rockin' with Alexander again. I imagined a painting that I could only fathom adding to my collection: one of Alexander and me dancing underneath the suspended deathly pale mannequins of the Coffin Club.

Just then Matt interrupted my daydream and gave Becky a peck on the neck—something I was desperately missing from Alexander.

Becky was right. I knew I'd see Alexander again—it was just a matter of when. But I was growing restless.

"I'd have thought you would have had that cleaned out days ago," Matt said. "Do you need help?"

"Thanks, but I want to savor this moment. I'll meet you guys out front."

As my favorite couple headed outside, a group of girls clutching designer purses and shoes passed by me like they were strutting down a catwalk, talking about European trips and boarding-school-style camps they'd be attending.

I just looked forward to the one place I *wouldn't* have to go—Dullsville High.

The warm summer air breezed through the open classroom doors and windows. I felt a few inches taller. I slung my backpack over my shoulder and briskly walked past the open classrooms.

I was just a few feet away from freedom. I reached out to push the main door open when someone jumped in front of me.

Nothing could spoil my mood today—not on my favorite day of the year. Well, almost nothing. Trevor Mitchell, lifelong nemesis and khaki-wearing thorn in my side, was staring down at me. "You didn't think I'd let you leave without saying good-bye?"

"Step aside before my boots make contact with your shins," I warned him.

"I haven't seen Monster Boy for weeks. Are you keeping him buried somewhere special?"

"Out of my way before I call the morgue. I think they have a vacancy."

"I'm really going to miss not seeing you every day." Trevor held his gaze a tad too long, like it had just hit him what he'd said. I could tell he was serious and it surprised him as much as it did me.

"I'm sure you'll get over it. You'll have your pick of uber-tanned *Baywatch* beauties to keep you busy."

"But what will *you* do? I heard Monster Boy left town. Forever. That will leave you in town all summer alone."

I hated that a rumor had started about Alexander being gone.

"He hasn't left . . . forever," I defended. "He's coming back. But it really doesn't matter because I'm going to see him. We're spending the summer together out of town and away from *you*."

I knew I was fibbing, but the thought of Trevor hanging out with lifeguards on each arm and mocking me while I waited alone at the Mansion made my mortal blood boil.

Trevor wasn't thwarted by my challenge. It only spurred him on.

"Then how about one kiss?" he said with a sexy grin. "Something to remember me by?" Though I had hints from Valentine of Trevor's inner desire for me, I was still suspect. I never knew what was going on in Trevor's head, much less his heart. I wasn't even sure he had one. Trevor was gorgeous—there was no doubt about it. His green melt-worthy eyes and his chiseled face could easily make him the next *Sports Illustrated* cover boy. But I was never sure if Trevor really liked me or just liked bullying me. Either way, he didn't move out of my way and instead leaned into me. There was only one guy I was going to kiss and that was Alexander.

I pushed my hand to his chest.

Trevor leered at me with a sexy grin. The more I fought back, the more he liked it. I was Trevor's ultimate soccer opponent and he was always desperate for one more game.

I paused for a moment and gazed up at the guy who'd tormented me since kindergarten. Trevor was really the only person who paid attention to me at school, besides Becky. I wasn't sure I wouldn't miss seeing him every day, too.

"I'll give you something to remember *me* by," I said. "The back of my head."

I pushed past him and escaped through the door to freedom.

I stepped out of Dullsville High and into the bright glare of the sun.

The year was behind me. Overall, it had been the best year of my life, for I'd met, dated, danced, and fallen in love with Alexander Sterling.

Students were walking home or getting into their daddies' overpriced luxury cars, heading off to begin their months of fun in the sun with people just like them. I'd spent a whole school year surrounded by people like Trevor.

My nemesis really forced me into seeing the light. It was time for me to be with people of my own kind. I wasn't going to spend my summer sans Alexander, much less another day.

There was only one thing keeping me and Alexander apart now. Me.

And that could easily be fixed with just a phone call.

Deadhead

More than a few months ago I'd waved good-bye to my mother at Dullsville's Greyhound bus stop and boarded the Hipsterville-bound bus to visit my ultra-conservative father's hippie sister, Aunt Libby.

Today I was on a Prozac high, minus the Prozac, ecstatic to return to the funky town of Hipsterville—home to unique coffee shops, with handmade coffee mugs and fresh scones (not the overincorporated cutout kinds with focus-group canned-in music), goth and hipster boutiques, and the perfectly morbid Coffin Club. I was excited to see Aunt Libby again, but even more important, I was only a few hours away from being reunited, or so I hoped, with my number-one vampire-mate.

I passed the bus ride doodling in my Olivia Outcast journal, imagining my reunion with Alexander. We'd meet inside the Coffin Club, where pale mannequins with bat wings hung from the ceiling and ghostlike fog permeated the air. Alexander would be waiting for me in the middle of the packed dance floor, with a single black rose. I'd run into his arms and he'd envelop me in them like a gothic Juliet. He'd lean into me and greet me with a long, seductive kiss, sending chills from my head to my combat boots. We'd dance the night away to the twisted sounds of the Skeletons until my legs could no longer hold me up. Alexander and I would venture off into a tiny church's graveyard, and we'd climb into a vacant crypt, where an empty coffin would be awaiting us. He'd close the lid on our night as dawn approached, and we'd snuggle together in darkness.

I was halfway through an episode of *The Munsters* on Billy Boy's borrowed (or rather bribed) iPod when I noticed the two-mile exit sign for Hipsterville.

Last time I arrived in Hipsterville, sunny skies and puffy blue clouds hung over the town. This time I was met with ominous clouds and a fierce downpour.

I covered myself with my skull-and-crossbones hoodie as the driver, undeterred by the pouring rain, unloaded suitcases from the bus's cargo hold. Finally I saw my suitcase, grabbed it, and huddled underneath the bus-stop shelter along with a crowd of other passengers. One thing hadn't changed—Aunt Libby was nowhere to be found.

I watched as each traveler was picked up by their party until I was the only traveler left waiting at the stop. When tapping my boots in the rising puddles grew boring, I headed for the convenience store a few yards away. I checked the aisles for any hippie chicks with the scent of potpourri or women wearing Nairobi sandals and tie-dyed skirts. Unfortunately, all I saw were a few truckers and the hungry bus driver.

I grew more excited to see my hipster Aunt Libby again. She and I were outsiders among the Madison clan. My aunt lived an unconventional lifestyle, working as a waitress in a vegan restaurant to support her acting career. She was a free spirit, and Hipsterville was a funky town where she could be her organic-eating, hemp-wearing, liberal self. Though we had different tastes, I always felt bonded with her in that we shared a passion for being different.

Ten minutes later, Aunt Libby was still nowhere to be found. Perhaps she was stuck in a rehearsal or filling up the saltshakers at the restaurant. I could feel the glare of the tattooed cashier. I didn't want to appear to be loitering, which I was, or stealing, which I wasn't. My stomach started to growl. I hovered over the candy aisle, debating which sugary cavity-forming candy to buy, when I felt a tap on my shoulder. I turned around. A beautiful lady wearing pressed pants, a Happy Homes real estate jacket, and my dad's smile was standing in front of me.

"Aunt Libby?" I asked, confused.

"Raven! It's great to see you!" She gave me a hard squeeze and I could feel her rain-stained face against my own dampened one. "I hope I wasn't too late."

"I just got here," I fibbed.

"I bet you're starved. We can stop and grab a bite. I took the rest of the day off." She lifted my suitcase and we hurried into her vintage Beetle.

I couldn't help but stare at my aunt, who had traded her waitress outfit for a real estate one, as we buckled in.

"Surprised to see me in a suit?" she asked, obviously reading my thoughts.

"I don't think I've ever seen you without sandals and a flower in your hair," I teased.

"I figured it was time to get a real job," she confessed. "I didn't bother telling your father. I haven't been working that long and I've already taken a half day." She laughed. "So who knows how much longer it will last."

She started the car and the engine putt-putted as she motored through the historic downtown area.

Aunt Libby was such an independent spirit, I felt disappointed and sad that she was giving up her dream. I didn't want her to change, nor did I ever want to change. I wondered, if Aunt Libby had to give up her passions, would I have to, too?

"Have you given up acting?" I asked.

"No, it's in my blood," she said. "In fact, I'm doing a one-woman show. You can take the girl out of acting but not the acting out of the girl."

I felt relieved. "A one-woman show . . . That's great. Soon enough you'll have your own Oscar."

Aunt Libby chuckled, then turned serious. Raindrops pelted the windshield and the rustic wipers struggled to clear them as we headed toward her apartment.

Something felt strange as I gazed out the window. An eerie shadow blanketed the town as we drove through it. I thought I saw a few bats hovering over a church.

"Wow . . . Those look like . . ."

"Bats?"

"Yes."

"There was a nest of them in one of the houses we have on the market. You would have loved it!"

"Awesome."

"And you would have loved this house we just rented."

"Really? Is it spooky?"

"Completely. It was a half-dead manor house."

"A manor house?" I asked. It couldn't have been the one Alexander and Jameson had occupied last time I was here.

"Yes," my aunt replied.

"Well, there must be a lot in this town," I hinted.

"Not too many. And not one like this."

"What do you mean?"

"It had been abandoned for years. The back lawn was completely overgrown, and I think the floors needed to be rehabbed, but the new renter didn't seem to mind."

"Is it the one on Lennox Hill Road?"

"Yes. How would you know?"

"Uh . . . I remember seeing pictures of it in the paper the last time I was here," I lied.

"It does seem like a house you would love to live in. I wouldn't be surprised if it was haunted."

If someone had rented the manor house, then where were Alexander and Jameson staying? And how would I ever find them?